Alec hesitated a moment, and then continued.

"Jillian, we're having a family barbecue at my parents' house this weekend—would you be willing to come with us? Me and Shelby?"

She caught her breath, knowing that if she agreed to go there would be no hiding their relationship. This was Alec's way of including her in the warm embrace of his family. Was she ready for this step?

Yes. Absolutely. "I'd love to." Jillian realised she'd just taken a gigantic step toward admitting to the world how she felt about him. Doubts instantly assailed her, and she pushed them away with determination.

There was really no reason she couldn't have it all. A career and a family. A beautiful stepdaughter.

And, most importantly, Alec's love.

BACHELOR DADS
Single Doctor… Single Father!

At work they are skilled medical professionals, but at home, as soon as they walk in the door, these eligible bachelors are on full-time fatherhood duty!

These devoted dads still find room in their lives for love…

It takes very special women to win the hearts of these dedicated doctors, and a very special kind of caring to make these single fathers full-time husbands!

BRIDE FOR A SINGLE DAD

BY
LAURA IDING

MILLS & BOON®

First published in Great Britain 2007
Harlequin Mills & Boon Limited,
Eton House, 18-24 Paradise Road, Richmond, Surrey TW9 1SR

© Laura Iding 2007

ISBN-13: 978 0 263 19807 2

Set in Tin
15-0607-4

Printed and bound in Great Britain
by Antony Rowe Ltd, Chippenham, Wiltshire

Laura Iding loved reading as a child, and when she ran out of books she readily made up her own, completing a little detective mini-series when she was twelve. But, despite her aspirations for being an author, her parents insisted she look into a 'real' career. So the summer after she turned thirteen she volunteered as a Candy Striper and fell in love with nursing. Now, after twenty years of experience in trauma/critical care, she's thrilled to combine her career and her hobby into one—writing Medical Romances™ for Mills & Boon®. Laura lives in the northern part of the United States, and spends all her spare time with her two teenage kids (help!), a daughter and a son, and her husband. Enjoy!

Recent titles by the same author:

HIS PREGNANT NURSE
THE DOCTOR'S CHRISTMAS PROPOSAL
THE FLIGHT DOCTOR'S ENGAGEMENT*
THE CONSULTANT'S HOMECOMING
A PERFECT FATHER
THE FLIGHT DOCTOR'S EMERGENCY*

Air Rescue

This book is dedicated
to my sister-in-law, Marianne Iding.
Thanks for being such a great friend.

CHAPTER ONE

Dr. Jillian Davis kept her head high, hopefully portraying a confidence she didn't feel as she strode through the emergency department at Trinity Medical Center.

"You're late." Dr. Wayne Netter, one of her colleagues, glared at her from his arrogant stance behind the arena nurses' station.

She ignored him, refusing to explain she was late as a result of her MRI scan being delayed. Her personal problems were none of his business. Impervious to his glare, she eyed the list of patients written on the whiteboard. "I see we have a full house."

"There's a couple of trauma victims on the way in," Luanne, the charge nurse, piped up. "Multiple gunshot wounds. ETA less than two minutes."

"Maybe I should stick around, in case you need help." Wayne Netter suffered from delusions of grandeur, acting as if he was the backbone of the emergency department, which was why he could barely tolerate knowing Jillian had been chosen for the role of interim medical director over him.

She raised a brow. "Sure, if you like. Although it's Friday night, and I wouldn't want to hold up your plans."

Wayne's gaze narrowed and she imagined he was already internally debating with himself. Was it more important she believe he had big plans on a Friday night or that she needed his dubious expertise for two simultaneous traumas?

Decisions, decisions. She fought a smile, especially when Luanne comically rolled her eyes from behind Wayne's back. Neither one of them particularly cared for the guy.

Clearing her throat, she turned her attention to Luanne. "Any other patient-care issues I need to know about?"

"Nope." Luanne shot a quick glance at Dr. Netter and belatedly Jillian realized Wayne might take her innocent remark as something derogatory. She stifled a sigh as Luanne hastened to assure her, "Everything's fine. The hospital beds are still pretty full and we have a few patients waiting on discharges upstairs."

"Great. I'll head over to the trauma room, then." Jillian walked away, feeling Wayne's piercing gaze boring into her back. To make a bad situation worse, she'd also once turned down his offer to go out for dinner, and he'd been impossible to deal with ever since. He just couldn't believe she wasn't interested. Of course, he didn't realize she hadn't dated a lot of guys in her lifetime. At first because her mother had been ill and later because she just hadn't found anyone interesting enough.

Wayne did not even come close to tempting her. When he didn't follow, she figured he'd decided not to stick around after all.

Breathing a sigh of relief, she focused her attention on the ED nurses and techs scurrying around to prepare the rooms for the incoming traumas. Sirens wailed from the ambulance bay and in moments the double doors burst open, spewing chaos into the room.

"John Doe number one, approximately sixteen years old with a gunshot wound to the belly, normal saline running wide open through two anticubital peripheral lines." A paramedic called out pertinent information as the patient was wheeled into the first trauma bay.

"John Doe number two, approximately the same age at sixteen, was shot in the chest. We intubated him in the field but his vitals are deteriorating rapidly. Fluids going wide open through two peripheral antecubital IVs."

Of the two, the chest wound was by far the more serious and required immediate attention. Jillian raised her voice. "Call for a cardiovascular surgery consult, stat."

"We already did, when the call about a gunshot wound to the chest first came in," Bonnie, one of the trauma nurses, quickly explained. "They were finishing up in surgery and planned to send a surgeon down."

"I don't see anyone yet. Call them again," Jillian ordered.

Another nurse picked up the phone to send a second page.

"Blood pressure barely 70 systolic and heart rate irregular and tachy at 120," Bonnie called out. "Looks like he may be trying to go into a wide complex rhythm."

Jillian wasn't surprised to see one of the paramedics kneeling on the gurney beside the second victim, keeping pressure on the chest wound. As the nurses fell into their respective roles on each side of the gurney, she donned sterile gloves and moved closer to examine the severity of the wound.

"Thanks, I have it now." She waved a hand, indicating he could let up on the wound. A flash of silver on a badge caught her eye and belatedly she realized the man holding pressure wasn't a paramedic at all but a cop.

He released pressure and immediately blood pooled in the center of the young man's chest. The cop slammed his hands back down, covering the gaping wound and leaning his weight over the area. "Dammit, he's going to bleed to death before the surgeon gets here."

Jillian couldn't argue—the brief glimpse she'd had of the injury told her it was bad. She snapped out orders. "I want four units of O-negative blood running through both IVs for a total of eight units, using the rapid infuser. Get this kid's blood pressure up before we lose him. I also want a portable suction unit here so I can examine this wound."

Marianne, another nurse, wheeled over a suction unit. Grabbing a pack of sterile gauze off the instrument table, Jillian turned back to the patient. She glanced up at the cop, registering a flash of recognition as she met his intense dark green eyes. "Let up on the wound again and this time stay off."

His expression grim, he nodded.

When he lifted his hands she shoved the sterile end of the suction catheter into the area to clear most of the blood. Using the gauze to soak up the remaining blood, she examined the wound.

"The bullet must have gone through the pericardial sac and injured his heart." The injury to the boy's chest was bad, but he had youth on his side. The young could survive a lot more than your average older adult. "Where's the surgeon?"

"He's on the way," Bonnie responded.

"Blood pressure continuing to drop despite the blood transfusions," Marianne informed her in a terse tone. "We'll need to start CPR."

"Give me another minute." Jillian continued sucking the blood from the wound, and then carefully packed the area with gauze, hoping to buy the kid a little more time.

"Dr. Raymond from CT surgery is here."

Finally.

"We lost his pressure!" Marianne cried.

No! Jillian stared at the monitor then glanced down at the boy. "Start CPR."

The cop still kneeling on the gurney placed his hands over the center of the kid's chest and began giving chest compressions. Blood continued to seep from the wound. She didn't waste time telling him to get down—for one thing the strength of his compressions were better than most, and for another, if they didn't fix the hole in this kid's heart soon, their efforts would be futile anyway.

"A bullet punctured the pericardial sac and grazed his myocardium." Jillian quickly gave the surgeon the details. "He'll need to go to the OR."

Todd Raymond shook his head as he glanced at the vital signs displayed on the heart monitor. "It's no use. He won't make it to the OR, he's lost too much blood."

Jillian couldn't believe his caviler attitude. Was he really going to give up that easily? She held onto her temper with an effort. "Are you telling me you're not even going to try?"

He shrugged. "What do you want me to do—open his chest here?"

"Get the chest tray, stat!" Jillian knew their efforts might be useless but this was a teenager, for heaven's sake! Didn't this child deserve every chance possible? "I'll give him some sedation."

When the tray was open and ready, the cop stopped giving compressions and jumped down from the gurney, knowing without being told that his assistance was no longer needed.

The alarm on the monitor overhead went off as the kid's heart rhythm went straight line without the aid of CPR. Jillian wasn't a surgeon but she didn't flinch when Todd drew his scalpel down the center of the boy's chest, meeting up with the open area left by the bullet.

"Hand me MacMillan forceps," Todd said as he opened the ribs to inspect the damage to the boy's heart.

She did as he asked, but at that moment the fingers of her right hand went numb and tingly, causing her to drop them. For a split second her horrified gaze met the cop's. Good thing the forceps had dropped onto the sterile field. She quickly picked them up again and handed them over.

"His left ventricle is severely damaged," Todd muttered as he used the forceps to trace the path of the bullet. Jillian stuck more gauze into the blood-filled cavity. "The right lung is also a mess—the bullet tore through both the middle and upper lobes."

"Try open heart massage," Jillian demanded. "Maybe if we can get his blood circulating long enough to get him on the heart-lung bypass machine…"

Todd Raymond did as she asked and massaged the heart, coaxing it back to some semblance of normal function, but even as they all stared at the straight line where the heart rhythm should have been on the monitor, she knew it was too late.

"It's over." Todd removed his hands from the kid's chest

and turned away. "I'm sorry. But with the injuries he'd sustained, his chance of survival was less than five percent."

He wasn't a percentage, he was a child! She wanted to scream, rant and rave at the tragic death but held herself in check. This boy wasn't the first patient she'd lost and unfortunately she doubted he'd be the last. She opened and closed the fingers of her right hand, trying to shake off the strange sensation. "Thanks for coming down, Todd."

"Sure." The surgeon stripped off his bloody gown and gloves, tossed them in the red-trash bag and left.

Jillian forced herself to turn her attention to the team of personnel working over the first victim. She'd left her senior resident in charge, using her expertise on the sicker of the two patients. "How are things going, Jack?"

"Fine. He's stable. The trauma surgery team is taking him to the OR to repair the damage to his intestines." Jack Dempsy seemed to have everything under control. As she watched, the surgeons packed up the gurney and wheeled John Doe number one away.

"Good." At least they hadn't lost them both. Losing one young man was bad enough.

When she turned back to the first victim, she saw the cop still standing there, staring down at the kid, seemingly unaware of the nurses who were clearing equipment out of the way.

When Marianne moved to pick up the remains of the boy's bloody shirt and pants, the cop held out his hand. "I'll take those."

Marianne glanced at Jillian for confirmation and she nodded, granting her permission. The nurse dropped the bloody clothes in a plastic bag and handed them over. He took the bag absently, staring at the boy, not appearing to be in a huge hurry to leave.

Now that the heat of the emergency was over, she cast through her memory for the cop's name. Alex? No, Alec. That's right. Alec Monroe. He'd come in about two months ago with a serious knife wound slashed diagonally across his flank requiring a good twenty-five stitches.

Embarrassed at how she'd remembered his name over the dozens of other patients she'd treated over the past few weeks, she wished she could slink away, especially knowing he'd seen the way she'd dropped the forceps. Did he wonder what was wrong with her? Or had he attributed the action to pure clumsiness?

"Thanks for going above and beyond with him," Alec said in a low tone, still staring at the dead victim.

"I'm sorry we couldn't do more."

He raised his gaze to hers, and her heart fluttered stupidly in her chest when she noticed he'd recognized her as well. His mouth quirked in a half-hearted smile. "Not your fault, Dr. Davis. He had the best doctor in the state as far as I'm concerned."

She felt her cheeks warm and inwardly cursed her fair skin. The cop had made her blush two months ago, too, teasing her as she'd stitched his wound. He was tall, well over six feet, and wore his chocolate-brown hair long and shaggy. She remembered his body was pure solid muscle. She'd been more aware of him than had been proper when taking care of a patient.

Opening and closing her hand again, she reminded herself to maintain her professionalism. "I hope your wound is all healed…"

"Sure." His smile disappeared. "I only wish these two kids had tried to settle their dispute with a knife instead of a gun. Then this kid might have had a chance."

"I know." She understood what he was saying. Once she would have argued that violence was violence regardless of the weapon of choice, but the crime rate in Milwaukee, Wisconsin had been climbing over the past few years and so had the use of guns. As a result, they'd treated more and more victims of gunshot wounds, many of them fatal.

Like this poor boy.

"Thanks again, Dr. Davis." Alec flashed a crooked smile.

Call me Jillian, she wanted to say, then realized the urge was inappropriate so she gave a brief nod instead. "You're welcome."

Alec turned away, heading for the door. Jillian watched him walk away, hoping she wouldn't have a reason to see him as a patient in the emergency department any time soon.

Cops like Alec put their lives on the line every day just to protect the innocent. To protect the public. People like her.

She couldn't imagine a more thankless job.

Or a more dangerous one.

Yet from the little she'd seen of him, between this visit and the previous one where he'd been cut with a knife, he seemed to thrive on his role, throwing his whole heart and soul into his career. Not many cops would have held pressure on a bleeding chest wound like he had.

Jillian shrugged off her troubled thoughts. Tucking her hands into the pockets of her lab coat, she spun on her heel to head back into the arena. No reason to worry about Alec—she had enough problems of her own.

Like how long would she have to wait to hear the results of her MRI?

And did she even want to hear the results?

Her gut instincts shouted no, even though she knew it was better to find out the truth now so she could figure out the potential impact on her career. Her stomach clenched in fear. She knew firsthand, after caring for her mother, just how badly this could affect her future. Although likely not for years yet.

Small comfort.

"Dr. Davis?"

Surprised, she glanced over her shoulder. A deep frown furrowed Alec's forehead as he strode back toward her.

"Yes?" She pivoted and waited for him to reach her.

"Do you have a minute?" His eyes, the color of jade, mesmerized her.

Her heart thudded in her chest. She should say no because, heaven knew, the arena was full of patients who might need her attention. But she found herself nodding her consent. "Of course. Is something wrong?"

"You could say that. I pulled these out of the kid's pants pocket." Alec's mouth thinned in a grim line as he held the items up for her to see.

"Percocets?" She frowned when she saw the individually wrapped packages of narcotics. "Was he recently hospitalized?"

Alec cocked his head questioningly. "Do medications come individually wrapped like this when you fill a prescription?"

"No." The implication of what he was telling her hit with the force of a brick. "You're saying those were stolen? From a hospital or clinic?"

"Yes." His gaze didn't waver from hers. "Would you know if anyone around here or anywhere else recently reported missing narcotics?"

Jillian opened her mouth and then closed it again without saying anything. Because the answer was yes.

Less than a week ago, twelve percocet tablets, just like the kind Alec held in his hand, had been discovered missing from the locked narcotic drawer right here in Trinity Medical Center's ED.

CHAPTER TWO

ALEC'S stomach clenched as he and Dr. Jillian Davis stared at the individually wrapped percocet tablets lying across the palm of his hand. He'd pulled these out of the sixteen-year-old John Doe's pocket, but for all he knew the kid had been selling them on the street to other kids. Younger ones. He'd found the young victims in Barclay Park after all. The idea of a child, like his six-year-old daughter Shelby, taking drugs of any kind made him feel sick.

"We can't discuss this here," Jillian said in a low tone. "Give me a minute to check on the status of our patients in the arena and then we can meet in my office."

Alec gave a tight nod, trying to remain calm. Thoughts of anything happening to Shelby haunted him. He'd only known about his daughter for the past year, when Shelby's mother had died and left a letter granting him custody. If he had known about Shelby sooner he would have been a part of her life from the beginning. Still, he was more than grateful he had his daughter now. Shelby had changed him for the better. He was more relaxed now, less intense.

Less lonely.

He and his daughter—the words still gave him a tiny

thrill—had grown close over this past year. Seeing kids as victims was doubly hard now. He knew his heightened awareness was due to Shelby. He couldn't imagine anything happening to his daughter.

Shelby was safe for today, though, in his sister Alaina's care. Alaina was the sensible sibling in the family. Not the wild Monroe, like he had once been. He trusted his older sister with his life.

Shelby was his life.

Swallowing hard, he closed his hand over the individually wrapped pills and followed Jillian from the trauma room into the arena. He slid the evidence into his pocket and stood off to the side. To take his mind off the seriousness of the situation, he concentrated on watching the pretty doctor in action.

Jillian looked over a clipboard with one of the nurses, no doubt to review each patient's planned disposition. Alec knew more than he wanted to about how emergency departments functioned. His brother Adam was a doctor and his younger sister Abby was a nurse, and at one point he'd been trained as a medic in the army with thoughts of following a similar career path.

Unfortunately, healing wasn't his area of expertise.

Maybe that wasn't entirely true, he amended. He'd helped to heal Shelby's loss. When she'd first come to live with him she'd cried all the time, the sound of her quiet sobs breaking his heart. Now she hugged him easily and called him "Daddy" without hesitation.

A reluctant smile quirked the edge of his lips.

Maybe Shelby had helped heal him, too.

He fingered the pills in his pocket. Had the flight

between the two teenagers been over the drugs? Or a girl? Or something else entirely?

He didn't know. But either way he couldn't do anything to bring the kid back, much as he wished he could. Shoving thoughts of the dead boy aside, his gaze followed Jillian's lithe figure as she entered a patient's room.

A few moments later she emerged from behind the curtain and returned to the nurses' station. His gaze lingered on her, the cute way her forehead puckered in a slight frown as she reviewed a patient's chart. Her serious expression made him wish he could make her laugh. Her hair, a rich chestnut color, was pulled back into a curly ponytail and he wondered how she'd look with her hair down, framing her face.

When he'd been brought into Trinity's ED after one of his suspects had tried to slice him with a knife, he'd been thankful the pretty doctor had been assigned to take care of him. As she'd tended his wound he'd been hyper-aware of her dainty yet capable hands on his skin. For the first time since Shelby had come to live with him, he'd considered asking a woman out.

Luckily, it had been a fleeting thought. His life was complicated enough, he didn't need to add another element that might disrupt Shelby's newfound peace.

He straightened from the wall when Jillian walked toward him. Despite his mini-lecture to himself, his body responded when he caught a whiff of her scent. "Alec? My office is this way."

She'd remembered his name. Stupid to be flattered, but he was. She led him to a tiny, compact office without so much as an outside window and waved him toward a seat as she settled in behind the modest desk.

Her medical school diplomas were framed and hung in prominent display on the wall behind her head. The reality of her extensive education punched him in the gut. Pretty as she may be, it was obvious Dr. Jillian Davis existed in a world very different from his.

"Could I see those percocets again?" Jillian asked. "I need to check the lot number."

He dug into his pocket and drew out the evidence. He tossed them onto her desk. "Why? So you can match the lot number to that of the drugs missing from this hospital?"

"Yes, but I'm not sure if hospital administration would approve of me discussing the details with you," Jillian admitted. She turned over the package and jotted a series of numbers on a pad of paper. "I think it's best if I get you in touch with our risk management department."

Alec frowned. He would have preferred to work with Jillian directly. In his experience, once hospital administrators were involved, the lines of communication became far less direct.

He leaned forward, pinning Jillian with a sharp gaze. "Dr. Davis, I really don't have time to mess around with your hospital administration. First of all, it's past seven on a Friday night and I'm sure most of the administrative staff has already gone home. If you make me wait until Monday, the trail will be cold. A sixteen-year-old kid died after exchanging gunfire with another, who is right now undergoing surgery. I need to know if these drugs cost this boy his life. Or, even worse, if other innocent kids are in danger."

She worried her lower lip between her teeth and a shot of desire stirred his groin. Dammit, he needed to stop thinking of the pretty doctor as an attractive woman. He had more important issues to deal with than his sudden awareness of a member of the opposite sex.

Not just any member of the opposite sex. Jillian was a doctor, with years of education and training behind her. He'd admired the way she'd managed the situation in the trauma room, taking charge, confronting the apathy of the surgeon on call.

Which reminded him of the moment when the forceps had dropped from her fingers. Jillian hadn't seemed like the clumsy type. He wasn't a doctor, but from where he stood it had looked as if she'd suddenly lost feeling in her fingers.

"There's six tablets here," Jillian murmured as she stared down at the percocets. "A week ago, there were twelve tablets of percocets missing from the narcotic cabinet."

"Twelve?" Alec forced his attention to the facts she was giving him. "So it's not just a couple of pills here and there?"

Jillian shook her head. "No. The timeframe from when the drugs were restocked until the time they were noticed as missing was almost three hours. At first the nurses thought maybe the pharmacy tech who stocked the drawer had miscounted, but when they questioned him, he was adamant that he hadn't made a mistake. The nurse who signed off on the tech's stocking of the drawer also verified the medication was there. A few people went into the machine for medication, but then cancelled their transaction. Management thinks maybe one of those nurses went in to take the pills and didn't record it, but the nurses swore they didn't take them and there's no proof one of them did. For now they're downloading information from the computer every day, watching for more trends."

"So the narcotics are locked in a computerized system?" he asked, grabbing that tidbit of information.

"Yes."

Interesting. He would have loved to see the machine for himself, but first things first. He took a small notebook out of his pocket. "Which nurses canceled their transactions?"

She hesitated. "I really think you should get the information from hospital administration. For all we know, someone may have gotten the password of one of these nurses. They could be innocent."

"Well, then, I'll take a list of all the nurses who were working that day."

Jillian looked apologetic. "The ED nurse manager, Rose Jenkins, gathered all the information together for the risk management department. I don't have the list, you'll have to get it from her." His concern must have shown on her face, because she quickly added, "I'd like to help you, but I really need clearance from hospital administration. There's usually someone on call." His nerves tingled when her fingertips brushed against his in the process of handing the percocets back to him. "I just can't believe this is a coincidence."

No, he didn't believe in coincidences either. As Jillian toyed with her pen, his two-way radio let out a squawk. His partner was no doubt trying to figure out what had happened to him.

He spoke quietly into the microphone and then stood. Jillian—no, Dr. Davis, he quickly amended—glanced up at him. "You need to go?"

"I'm afraid so." He didn't bother to hide the pang of regret. "Would you mind if I called you tomorrow? Are you working?"

"I'm not working but you can always reach me on my pager, I wear it twenty-four seven." Jillian rose to her feet and handed him a slim, white business card. "Give me a few hours tomorrow morning to page the administrator on call. I'll do my best to help you."

"Great." He stared at the number on the embossed card, understanding her commitment to her job was as deeply ingrained as his. Was she married? Did she have children, too? For some reason, and not just her ringless fingers, he thought not. "Thanks again, Dr. Davis." He moved toward the door.

"Alec?" The husky way she said his name sent goose-bumps down his arms.

"Yes?" He turned toward her, steeling himself against the surge of awareness.

"Please, call me Jillian." Her smile held a note of un-certainty.

Despite his efforts to keep his distance, warmth seeped through his chest at her request. "Pretty name, Jillian." He couldn't help grinning when she blushed and he slid her card into his breast pocket. "I'll talk to you tomorrow."

"Sounds good."

He flashed her one last smile, before walking outside to meet his partner. The traitorous part of his body was looking forward to seeing Jillian again.

Work-related or not.

Jillian got up early as she usually did and went for a three-mile run. At least her legs seemed to be working all right, no signs of weakness there. Afterwards, she paged the hospital administrator on call. All she could do then was wait. After she showered and changed, she stood and stared at her closet, desperately searching for something to wear.

When she realized what she was doing, anticipating Alec's phone call, she turned away from the dressy clothes and grabbed the pair of comfortable jeans paired with a casual short-sleeved T-shirt she usually wore on her days off.

She probably wouldn't see Alec anyway, unless the hospital administrator called her back soon. Over an hour had passed and she hadn't gotten a response yet. Likely, she wasn't going to be able to help him after all.

Disappointed, she hoped Alec wouldn't be upset with her. Although why she cared if he was upset or not was beyond her. It wasn't as if she was going to see him on a regular basis or anything. Would she? Her heart gave an expectant leap until she squashed the sensation with common sense. No, of course not. Their paths wouldn't likely cross again.

The tingling sensation returned to her fingers. She stopped in her tracks and stared accusingly at her right hand. The numbness and tingling came and went without warning. Her initial doctor's appointment had been almost six weeks ago. The neurology specialist, Dr. Juran, had ordered a broad-spectrum lab panel, and thankfully the results had come back as normal. When her symptoms hadn't returned right away, she'd put off scheduling her MRI scan. Until Dr. Juran had called, urging her to get it done.

She'd had the MRI yesterday. She'd called to find out the results and had been told they wouldn't be available until Monday.

Dr. Juran had been noncommittal when she'd asked him about multiple sclerosis. Her mother had suffered from the auto-immune disorder. In the beginning, Angela Davis hadn't been slowed down much from her disease. Yet over time she had grown weaker and weaker until finally she hadn't been able to take care of herself. Since Jillian's father had died of a heart attack when she'd been in her early twenties, Jillian had been left to be the sole provider of care for her mother, until Angela had finally passed away as well.

Jillian caught her lower lip between her teeth. Dr. Juran had explained MS wasn't hereditary, so she needed to stop making herself crazy by thinking she had the same disease.

With a choppy sigh she flexed her fingers until the sensation passed. Like the last time, the symptoms didn't bother her for long. Just enough to make her aware something was wrong.

She tore her gaze from her hand. Obsessing over what she might have wasn't how she wanted to spend the weekend. She was lucky to have two whole days off. She needed to enjoy them.

And she would. Glancing at her watch, she tried to think of the best way to plan her day, considering all the various errands she had to run.

Maybe she should wait to leave until Alec had called.

Wait a minute, since when had she planned her life around a man?

Not since she'd been sixteen and infatuated with Steven Wade, the quarterback of the football team who hadn't known the bookworm-school-valedictorian had been alive.

With a determined motion, Jillian swept her purse off the counter, intent on heading outside to her car. The pager at her waist vibrated and, despite herself, she grasped the unit eagerly. The number flashing across the display wasn't the hospital's.

As she didn't have a personal life to speak of, the number had to be Alec's.

Her heart leaped in her chest. She turned and walked into the kitchen, dropping her purse back on the table. Taking a steadying breath, she picked up her phone and dialed the number.

"Alec Monroe," he said by way of greeting.

"Hi, Alec. This is Jillian, returning your call." She cursed the butterflies mating in her stomach. What in the world was wrong with her?

"Thanks for getting back to me so quickly." His deep voice held a note of warmth, unless she was totally imagining it. "Would you have time to go out for lunch?"

"Lunch?" She stared at the wall calendar and the blank space labeled Saturday, knowing full well she didn't have other plans. She wanted nothing more than to go, but Alec wouldn't be happy to hear she couldn't help him. "I'm sorry, Alec, but I haven't heard back from anyone in hospital administration yet."

"That's all right," he assured her. "I have something else I want to talk to you about."

"You do?" Her interest piqued, she quickly gave her consent. "Sure, I'd love to have lunch. Ah, where would you like to meet?"

He hesitated, and she sensed he wanted to argue about meeting at the restaurant, but was pleasantly surprised when he didn't. "Do you like Italian? We could meet at Giovani's, say, around eleven-thirty?"

"Giovani's is perfect. See you then, Alec."

Jillian hung up the phone, already shaking her head at her own foolishness. She was acting like a goof.

This wasn't a date. This really wasn't a date.

Ha! Maybe if she told herself that often enough, she'd figure out a way to believe it.

Alec wanted to ask her about something else. Like what? No doubt he had medical questions of some sort. A few of the men she'd dated in college had seemed to want to know all about various disease processes once they'd known she was a medical student.

She clutched her purse to her chest, feeling the same uncertainty she'd experienced back then, going out on her first date.

The guy had been nice enough, but their relationship hadn't gone anywhere. In fact, none of the men she'd dated on and off during her college years had evoked deep feelings on her part.

Maybe because none of them had been anything like Alec. Alec was different. He put his life on the line for others, yet oozed masculinity and sensual awareness in a way she'd never experienced before.

She couldn't deny that his magnetic attraction made her secretly thrilled to be seeing him again.

CHAPTER THREE

ALEC hated working weekends, not appreciating the way the job cut into his personal time with his daughter. He'd debated bringing Shelby along, but then Alaina had mentioned taking the kids to a water park and the excited glint in his daughter's eye had convinced him it was better for her to go with his sister. Beth, Alaina's daughter, was close to Shelby's age and the two of them had become almost inseparable over the past eight months.

The knowledge should have made him feel less guilty about working the weekend, but didn't.

He arrived at the restaurant early, having finished interviewing the neighbors around the area where the shooting had taken place sooner than he'd thought.

He stood in the shade of the building to wait for Jillian, seeking respite from the hot sun. The hours he'd spent gathering information hadn't revealed much about why the two boys had begun to fight, but his John Doe number two did have a name.

Richard James Dordan. Known by his friends as Ricky.

The kid had celebrated his sixteenth birthday three weeks

earlier. He'd played football and, according to his mother, had had dreams of qualifying for a college scholarship.

Ricky's mother didn't have any idea where he might have gotten the drugs. She claimed he'd been a good boy who hadn't gotten into trouble with the law or skipped school as much as the other kids did. Football had been too important to him.

He could have pointed out that good boys didn't usually carry guns and percocets but he hadn't. Because deep down he believed her. Ricky probably was a good kid, who had made the stupid mistake of trying to settle an argument with a gun.

Where Ricky had gotten the gun and the drugs was a complete mystery. Although Ricky's juvenile record did show he'd once run with a rough crowd.

He glanced up when a sedate blue Chevy Malibu pulled into the parking lot. When Jillian climbed out, his chest tightened and he nearly swallowed his tongue. She was dressed casually, in jeans that appeared to have been molded solely for her long legs and lean backside, paired with a tiny V-necked top that emphasized the high curve of her breasts. In the hospital her long white lab coat and conservative business clothes had given her a professional, hands-off image.

Now, with her hair falling in waves around her shoulders, Jillian looked young. Fresh. Beautiful. And close. Very close.

Well within reach.

"Hi!" Her breathless smile almost sent him to his knees. "I hope you weren't waiting long?"

He shook his head, trying to convince his lame brain not

to fail him, now. He pried his tongue from the roof of his mouth. "Not at all." He pulled the door open for her, somewhat surprised she wasn't driving something a little more fun and sporty. He could easily see her in a flashy convertible. "I finished up early."

"I'm hungry," she confided as they were seated at a cozy table for two. "I'm glad you suggested meeting for lunch."

"Me, too." He knew better than to think of a simple sharing of a meal as a date but it was a difficult fact to remember when he wanted nothing more than to kiss her. He pulled his gaze from the temptation of her mouth with an effort. Once seated, they pondered the menus and placed their orders. When they both chose the same Italian dish, she laughed.

He sucked in his breath. She went from beautiful to stunning when she laughed.

It didn't take much to imagine her smiling and laughing with his family. He came from a loud, noisy clan and he knew his parents and five siblings would love her. He suspected his youngest sister, Abby, especially would get on with Jillian.

Maybe he should invite Jillian to Abby and Nick's wedding next month?

Or not, as he already had a date. With his daughter.

"I'm sorry I can't be more helpful about your case, Alec," she said in a soft, apologetic tone. "But I promise as soon as Monday comes, I'll make sure you get the list of staff members you requested."

He shrugged, hiding his disappointment. He appreciated her need to go through proper channels, but it wasn't easy to hold off on the investigation when kids' lives were at

stake. "That's all right. I did want to ask you about something kind of related to the case." He flashed a chagrined
smile. "Percocets are pain pills, right?"

She nodded. "Yes."

"Can you think of any reason why a sixteen-year-old
would have them in his pocket?"

She sat back in her chair, tilted her head and drew her
brows together in a small frown. He liked the way she
carefully considered his questions, as if they were important. She didn't just give an easy answer off the top of her
head. "Not really, unless he'd recently had surgery, which
could be verified on autopsy. If not, I can only assume he
planned to sell them, but, from what I hear, percocets don't
have the same street value as other drugs, like oxycodone."

He raised a brow at her perceptiveness. "You're right
about that. I've asked questions and heard the same thing.
Still, it's unusual for kids to have this kind of drug. Our narcotics division has seen more marijuana or crack cocaine
or even heroin. Anything but percocets."

Jillian shivered. "I don't even like to think about any of
those drugs ending up in kids' hands."

Yeah, he was totally in sync with her on that one. The
image of Shelby's innocent smile flashed in his mind as
he added a heartfelt, "Me either."

"I guess I lived a pretty sheltered life," Jillian mused. "I
didn't know much about any of this stuff until I started
working in the ED."

Alec found himself wanting to know more about Jillian
Davis. He leaned forward. "Did you grow up here in
Milwaukee?"

"Yes." She shrugged a graceful shoulder. "My parents

were older when they had me, and they were a bit over-protective. As they were both college professors, I ended up spending a lot of time in classrooms. Not that I minded. I loved books."

"So you were good in school." He could easily see her, studying intently in the library.

"Good enough to be granted a college scholarship." She paused when the waiter brought their food to the table. "This looks delicious."

For a few minutes they concentrated on their respective meals. Alec glanced at her, his gaze drawn to her lovely face. She'd mentioned having a sheltered life and he could see how that might be the case. Heck, as far as he was concerned, Jillian shouldn't have to take care of any victims of drug abuse. He took a bite of his chicken marinara, wishing the ugly side of his job hadn't touched her. No one liked dealing with criminals at any level. Unfortunately, there was little he could do except continue his investigation and then hand over the details to his boss.

Which reminded him of one more thing. "At some point I'd like to see your medication dispensing machine."

"Stop by while I'm working and I'll show it to you," Jillian offered. "The way the machines work isn't a big secret and when you get the list from Administration, make sure you ask for the names of the staff members who accessed it during those time frames."

"I will. Thanks for the tip." The way Jillian dug into her pasta with gusto made him grin. He could appreciate a woman with a healthy appetite.

She was beautiful. Successful. Financially secure. He

hid a grimace. She probably made at least twice as much money per year as he did. She was way out of his league.

So what was he doing here, watching her eat? What was the point of fantasizing about asking her out again? If he had the chance, he'd take her out to a fancy restaurant for a nice, quiet dinner. One where she might agree to invite him to her place afterwards.

The phone at his waist chirped loudly. He glanced at the display, and then flashed Jillian an apologetic smile.

"Excuse me, this is my daughter." He opened his phone. "Hi, munchkin, what's up?"

"Daddy!" Shelby shrieked in his ear. "I slid down a water slide and my whole head went underneath the water!"

A moment of panic made him tighten his grip on the phone. "Are you all right? Are you hurt? Did you cry?"

"No, silly." To his relief she giggled. "I just held my breath. I didn't like it when water went up my nose, though."

Swimming lessons, he thought, relaxing one finger at a time from the death-like grip on his phone. Shelby needed swimming lessons, and fast. "You're supposed to blow air out your nose, so water doesn't come in."

"Ew. Gross." He chuckled, imagining the scrunched expression on her face. "Auntie Alaina is calling me so I have to go, Daddy. I love you."

His throat tightened. He'd never, ever get tired of hearing her say that. "I love you, too, Shelby. See you later." He cleared his throat as he snapped his phone shut.

Jillian stared at him, her eyes wide with shocked surprise. Then she pulled herself together, although he noticed her smile was strained. "Your daughter sounds adorable. How old is she?"

"Six. Almost seven." He tried to think of a way to explain without going into the whole complicated story. "She's only lived with me for the past year, since her mother died."

"Oh, I'm so sorry." Jillian's expression softened. "That must have been very difficult."

"Kids are incredibly resilient. Shelby seems to have adjusted fairly well. So have I. We make a pretty good team."

Jillian glanced away, making him realize he'd given the impression that he wasn't interested in expanding that team.

A fact he hadn't meant to state so boldly.

She reached for her water glass but as she lifted it, the stem slipped from her fingers and fell back onto the table. The glass didn't break, but a little water sloshed over the edge. "I'm such a klutz!" Jillian exclaimed as she leaned over to mop up the mess, avoiding his gaze. "And, actually, Alec, I'm sorry but I need to get going. I have a number of things I need to do today."

He couldn't let her go, not like this. Reaching across the table, he caught her hand. "Jillian, wait."

She froze, staring down at their joined hands. Then she looked up at him, her gaze uncertain. "For what?"

Stroking a thumb over the soft skin of her hand, he held her gaze. "You dropped the forceps in the ED and now this. Jillian, you're not a klutz. But you certainly seem upset. I hope you don't mind my asking, but is something wrong?"

There was a long pause, but then she tugged her hand from his. "I honestly don't know. But, really, I do need to get going. Please, excuse me." She picked up her purse. "Thanks for lunch, Alec. I hope you hear from the hospital administration soon so you can find the person you're searching for."

He watched her walk away, feeling bad about the abrupt way she'd pulled away from him. He also couldn't help wondering what was wrong. She'd said she didn't know but, as a physician, she must have an idea.

He signaled for the check, sternly reminding himself that Jillian's medical problems weren't any of his concern. His problem was to find the person stealing percocets from the hospital and putting them in the hands of children.

No way was he searching for anything on a personal level. Especially not a potential wife for himself or mother for Shelby.

Jillian spent the rest of her weekend trying to wrench the image of Alec talking to his daughter out of her head. She had thought him an attractive man before she'd known about his daughter. Yes, it had been a bit of a shock to find out he was a dad, but seeing him in his sensitive caring mode had made trying to pry him out of her mind even harder.

Reading professional medical journals helped to a certain extent, because there was always so much to learn. After a couple of hours, though, her mind drifted back to Alec. Disgusted, she considered calling the ED to see if they needed additional help. Anything was better than sitting around, dwelling on her lack of a personal life.

Especially when the void hadn't bothered her until now.

When her phone rang early Saturday evening, she was surprised and just a little disappointed when the caller was one of her colleagues, Craig Bartlet.

"Hey, Jillian. Would you do me a favor?"

"Sure." At the moment she would have agreed to almost anything. "What do you need? Someone to cover your shift?"

"Sort of. Trinity Medical Center and Children's Memorial Hospital are sponsoring the Festival of the Arts down at the lakefront this weekend. I'm supposed to be volunteering in the first-aid station tomorrow, but my son is sick. Would you mind taking my shift from one to four in the afternoon?"

"Sure." Helping out in the first-aid station didn't sound too hard. And besides, she didn't mind a little volunteer work.

"Thanks a lot, Jillian." Greg sounded relieved. "I owe you."

"No, you don't. It's not a big deal at all. Just take care of yourself and your son."

"I will."

The next day Jillian headed down to the lakefront early, so she could make sure to find a parking spot. The art museum was a beautiful modern white structure overlooking the shores of Lake Michigan. There were various art displays set up along the lakefront and she took a few minutes to browse through works by local artists before heading over to the small trailer with the universal red cross on the front.

There was a man and a woman inside. The guy looked somewhat familiar. He stepped forward. "Hi. Can I help you?"

"Yes. I'm Dr. Jillian Davis, I'm here to cover Craig's shift."

"Ah, that explains it. I didn't think you were Craig." His green eyes twinkled. "I'm Adam, and my shift is over." He glanced at the woman. "Mary, would you mind giving Jillian the rundown of how we're set up?"

"No problem." The woman smiled at her. "I'm Mary Drover, the person who's stuck here all day." She rolled her eyes at Adam when he laughed. "Thanks for helping out. When I'm not here, you can get in touch with me on this two-way radio."

"Nice meeting you, Jillian. See you later, Mary." Adam gave them both a little wave as he left the trailer.

Mary spent a few minutes showing her around. The trailer was set up very much like a mini-emergency room.

"All right, I'm going to walk around outside for a while," Mary told her. "Remember to call me if you need me."

Jillian nodded. She hadn't known what to expect from the first-aid station, but alone in the trailer, she looked around and thought maybe she should have brought something to read in order to keep busy.

It turned out her optimism was premature. Within ten minutes she heard a little boy crying and a young mother rushed in, her blouse smeared with blood. "My son Joey fell and hit the back of his head on the pavement."

"All right, let's take a look." Jillian indicated the mother should set Joey, who looked to be about five, on the small exam table. They boy was still crying and she tried to soothe him while she examined the back of his head. "There, now, Joey, it's all right. I know your head hurts, but you're fine now." Luckily the cut was pretty small, but there was some tissue swelling. "I don't think it needs stitches," she said to his mother. "But he does have a small lump here and I'd like to apply a cold pack."

"No stitches? Are you sure? There was so much blood!" The woman held onto the boy, trying to ease his crying.

"Head wounds bleed a lot, but we'll use the ice first and see how it goes." Jillian smiled at the boy as his sobs quieted to smaller hiccups. She cracked a cold pack and mixed the chemical contents to activate it before placing it on his head. "There now, you're so brave. How would you like a lollipop? If your mom says it's OK," she amended.

"Sure." Joey's mother appeared relieved when her son stopped crying and chose a grape sucker. "Thanks. I'm glad it's not serious."

"No, he should be fine." Jillian wondered if most of the patients she'd see during the afternoon would be children. She didn't really mind. Sometimes kids came into the Trinity Medical Center's ED by mistake, instead of going to Children's Memorial, which was right next door. She wasn't a pediatrician by trade, but she could handle kids if needed.

Her next patient proved her theory wrong, when a frail elderly lady came in, after nearly fainting in the heat.

Jillian managed to get the woman to drink some Gatorade and assessed her to make sure she wasn't having some sort of stroke or any other undiagnosed illness. However, after about thirty minutes, the woman seemed much better and Jillian allowed her to leave, although she cautioned her that if she became light-headed again to call 911.

"I will, dear. Thank you."

The trailer was quiet for another fifteen minutes before her door opened again.

"Jillian!"

She was just as surprised to see Alec, holding a young girl whose heart-shaped face was streaked with tears. "Alec. What's wrong?"

"Shelby's arm swelled up from a bee sting." He set his daughter on the exam table.

"Is she allergic?" Jillian asked, getting another cold pack ready.

"I don't know." Alec looked worried. "She's never been stung by a bee before. I figured we needed to come here just in case she needed some epinephrine."

Smart thinking on Alec's part. "Hi, Shelby, my name is Dr. Jillian." The girl's sobs had quieted to small sniffles. Gently taking Shelby's arm, she examined the large reddened area right above her elbow. "Do you remember what happened?"

"A bee kept flying near my soda." Shelby's tone indicated she despised the creatures. Jillian put the cold pack over the swollen area, trying to gauge if Shelby was showing other signs of an allergic reaction. Her breathing appeared good. "He wouldn't go away, then the next thing I knew, my arm burned."

"And you're sure you've never been stung before?" Jillian asked.

"I'm sure." Shelby's head bobbed up and down. Her dark brown hair was the exact shade of Alec's but the similarities stopped there. Shelby had big brown eyes, not sparkling green ones.

"Alec, the epi-sticks are in that right-hand drawer over there. Maybe grab one, just in case." Jillian held the cold pack on Shelby's arm, and Alec crossed over, to find the epi-sticks.

She wrapped a comforting arm around Shelby's shoulders. The little girl sighed and leaned her head against Jillian, as if the whole traumatic experience had worn her out.

Jillian soothed a hand over Shelby's hair, catching a whiff of baby shampoo. Alec's daughter was a cutie.

"What do you think?" Alec asked, his brows pulled together in a frown as he brought over the epi-sticks. "Is she allergic?"

"So far, so good." She flashed him a reassuring smile. Carefully, so as not to dislodge Shelby from resting against her, Jillian lifted the edge of the cold pack to assess the swelling. The reddened area didn't look any worse. "I don't think so, but we'd better keep an eye on it for a little while." Jillian waved a hand at the lollipops. "Do you mind if she has one?"

"No, I don't mind." Alec gave his daughter a curious look. "Shel, what flavor would you like? Cherry or grape?"

Shelby lifted her head from Jillian and pursed her lips. "Cherry."

"All right, then." He peeled off the wrapper and handed it to her.

She popped it into her mouth. "Thank you," she mumbled, her speech garbled from the sucker.

"You're welcome." Jillian watched Alec with his daughter and remembered he'd said something about Shelby only living with him for the past year, since her mother's death. She could only imagine how terrible that must have been for such a young girl.

"Why does the cold make the swelling go down?" Shelby wanted to know.

"Ah, good question." She tried to think of a non-complicated answer. "When you hurt yourself, your body tries to fix it by sending white blood cells to the area. Which is good, but too much swelling hurts, too."

Shelby scrunched up her forehead. "Doesn't the body know better than to send so many white blood cells?"

Jillian had to laugh. "No, not really." She lifted the corner of the cold pack again, keeping an eye on the clock. "See how much better it looks? The cold makes your veins close up and helps the body stop sending white blood cells to the area that hurts."

Shelby peered at the sting site in her arm. "It doesn't hurt very much either."

The cold pack had probably numbed the area. Jillian glanced at Alec. "You might want to give her some Benadryl tonight, before she goes to bed. The antihistamine will help counteract any bee serum left in her system."

"Benadryl," Alec repeated, his brows pulled together in a frown. "I'll have to buy some."

Jillian opened drawers to see if there were any samples. When she found a small packet of Benadryl, she handed it over. "Here you go."

"Thanks." He stepped closer to take the medication and his unique musky scent surrounded her. Suddenly, the small trailer seemed even more cramped, as his broad shoulders took up more than a little space. Now that Shelby's minor emergency was over, Jillian didn't know what to say.

Small talk had never been easy for her. She was more comfortable with books.

"Do you think we should head home?" Alec asked.

"No!" Shelby protested. "We didn't get to spend hardly any time in the children's tent."

"Children's tent?" Jillian wasn't sure what Shelby was talking about.

"I got the tickets to come here today from my brother Adam. He told me they have a children's tent where the kids can do finger-painting and stuff."

Adam? She made the connection. "Adam was here as one of the volunteers. I thought he looked familiar."

"I missed him? Figures." Alec glanced at Shelby. "Are you sure you want to stay?"

"Yes." Shelby gave a vigorous nod.

Jillian removed the cold pack, and took one last look at Shelby's arm. "The swelling has really come down. If you want to stay, it should be all right."

"All right, then." Alec glanced at her. "Thanks again, Jillian." He paused, and then added, "How long are you working?"

"Another hour or so," she said.

He nodded. "Maybe we'll see you later."

"Sure." Jillian knew he was just being polite.

Shelby happily jumped down from the exam table. "Bye, Dr. Jillian."

"Bye, Shelby. Have fun in the children's tent."

Alec took his daughter's hand as they left. He was a good father. And why that had suddenly become an attractive trait in a man was beyond her. Alec obviously cherished his daughter and the feeling was mutual.

Her memories of her own father were mostly centered around doing homework. He'd always been willing to help, showing great patience when it had come to her studies. Jillian had been an only child, and her parents had been in their early forties by the time she'd been born. They had viewed education as being highly important. Most of the other kids had had younger, more active parents, but Jillian hadn't really minded. She'd loved books and once she'd hit high school had fallen in love with science. She'd known then she was destined to become a doctor.

Her choices, sacrifices some would say, had never bothered her before. There was no reason for them to nag at her now. Her career was something she'd worked for. Having a family of her own just hadn't been a priority. Especially once her mother had gotten sick and her attention had been focused on caring for her mother, rather than her personal life.

Now she couldn't help but wonder what she'd missed. When Shelby had rested her head against her shoulder, she'd been struck by a flash of tenderness for the motherless girl. Never before had she been so tempted to gather a child into her arms for a big hug.

At the end of her shift, Jillian stepped from the trailer to find Alec and Shelby walking toward her. Alec's gaze was warm as he acknowledged her with a nod.

"Are you hungry? We were thinking of having barbequed spare ribs for dinner."

Pleased they'd thought of her, she nodded. "Sounds good."

They wandered over to where the food vendors were lined up along the edge of the festival grounds. Eating while talking wasn't easy, although Shelby didn't seem to have nearly the same problem as she chatted about their activities in the children's tent.

After they'd finished their impromptu meal, Alec insisted on walking her to her car. With Shelby right there between them, she understood when he didn't reach for her hand.

"Goodnight, Shelby.' She smiled at the tired little girl.

"Goodnight, Dr Jillian." Shelby gave her a beautiful smile, before yawning and rubbing her eyes.

"And, Alec." Jillian kept her tone light. "Thanks for dinner."

"Goodnight, Jillian." Alec's gaze met hers directly, and a sizzling awareness flashed between them. The glimpse of desire in his eyes convinced her she wasn't alone in feeling the attraction. "I may stop in to see you tomorrow."

Really? For a moment hope flared, until he added, "To get the list."

"Oh, yes. Of course." He was referring to the list of staff members she'd promised him. Work-related, not pleasure. Jillian unlocked her car and opened the door. "I'm working day shift tomorrow."

"Oh." Was that disappointment clouding his eyes? "Then I won't see you. I'm working second shift."

It was tempting to promise to work a double shift, just so she could see him. As Alec and Shelby walked away, Jillian couldn't hide a keen sense of disappointment.

She'd run into Alec today by chance. But once he had his list, her opportunities for seeing him again would dwindle to almost nothing.

CHAPTER FOUR

JILLIAN headed to the hospital bright and early the next morning, despite her restless night. It was all Alec's fault, she thought, feeling cranky as she walked in. Reliving those precious moments she'd spent with Alec and his daughter had made it impossible to fall asleep.

At least ignoring her fatigue was easier once she began seeing patients. What she loved most about the ED was the wide variety of illnesses and injuries. She was never bored—how could you be when you never knew what your day would bring?

At just before noon, one of the nurses, Susan Green, gestured her over. "Dr. Davis, you need to look at this patient. He's suffered a pretty severe second-degree burn on his arm."

"I'll be right there." Jillian quickly washed her hands before walking over to see the patient. She picked his clipboard up off the table to glance at his name and his vital signs. "Mr. Perry, my name is Dr. Davis. What happened? How did you burn yourself?"

"I was stupid," Mr Perry admitted, grimacing when she lifted an edge of the cold towel that had been placed over the burn to gauge the damage. "I was trying to burn some garbage and as it rained the other day, everything in the fire-pit was wet. So I thought I'd use a little lighter fluid…" He sucked in a breath when she lifted the towel all the way off and the air hit the raw skin. "Stupid. There was a small explosion. I dropped and rolled in the grass, then went to stand in a cold shower."

"Very smart," she told him. "Exactly the right treatment for a burn."

"Smart, yeah." Mr. Perry, a well-built man in his forties, snorted. "Not smart enough to avoid a dangerous short-cut."

"Maybe not, but this could be worse," Jillian admitted. The burned area covered almost the entire expanse of his arm between his elbow and his wrist. "You still have hair follicles, which means you won't need a skin graft. This burn will be painful, but once the area has healed, it shouldn't leave a scar."

"Good." His smile was wan.

She replaced the cool towel. "I'm going to have one of the nurses wash this up and put a dressing over it. We'll give you some percocets for the pain. You'll need someone to drive you home, though, if you take the pain medicine here."

"I'll hold off on the pain medicine for now. Otherwise I'll have to call my ex-wife," Mr. Perry said with a sigh. "She won't be happy with me."

Jillian flashed a sympathetic grin. "OK, but burns are painful. You may need to swallow your pride and call her."

"Jillian?" Luanne poked her head into the room. "You have a call on line one."

She gave her patient one last smile, then crossed over to grab the phone. "Hello, this is Dr. Davis."

"Jillian, Dr. Juran here. Do you have some time you could come and see me over the lunch hour? I'd like to discuss the results of your MRI scan."

Dr. Juran? Good grief, she'd forgotten all about her MRI results. Her stomach sank to her toes. She momentarily closed her eyes and braced herself. "I guess this means you can't tell me over the phone."

There was a slight pause on the other end of the line. "No. I don't want you to worry," he added, "but I really would rather see you in person."

His attempt to lighten the blow wasn't working. Knowing her fate was about to be sealed, she forced herself to speak. "I'll be right there."

She hung up and let Luanne know she was leaving.

"Are you all right?" Luanne asked in concern. The two of them had become good friends over the past year.

"I'm fine," Jillian lied, not wanting to go into the whole story right now. "Page me if you need something."

Down in Dr. Juran's office, she didn't wait for more than a few seconds before being escorted in.

"Jillian, please, sit down."

She did, mostly because her knees went weak.

"Your MRI was normal. However, you need to understand there is a small chance you could still have MS or some other auto-immune disorder."

Her MRI results were normal? The relief faded all too quickly as the rest of his comments sank into her surprised brain. "A small chance? Like how small?"

"Five percent." Dr. Juran, a fatherly man in his late fifties, took one of her hands reassuringly in his. "I would like to do one more test, Jillian. Evoked potentials."

She tried to keep her expression neutral but inside her stomach clenched. "I've heard they're painful."

He gave a solemn nod, his gaze apologetic. "I won't lie to you. It isn't a comfortable procedure. We can't give you medication to relax you because the purpose of the test is to stimulate the nerves. We can't take away the pain."

"I understand." She stared at him. "Do you really think there's something wrong with me?"

He didn't answer for a long moment. Then his tone was gentle. "Jillian, as a physician yourself, you're aware there is still so much about the body, specifically the nervous system, that we don't know. Obviously you have symptoms that are being caused by something. But I think you are borrowing trouble by expecting the worst. I've told you before, MS isn't genetic. It's caused by a virus that settles for some reason in the myelin tissue surrounding your nerves."

Yes, she knew that much. She'd read everything she could about the disease when her mother had grown ill.

He squeezed her hand. "Please, try not to worry. We'll run some more tests and keep an eye on you. As long as your symptoms don't grow worse, there's no need to panic. At this point, your symptoms are mild enough to hold off on treatment anyway."

She took a deep breath and let it out slowly. He was right. She was making this entire situation worse than it needed to be. "All right. I'll try not to worry. Five percent is a pretty low number."

Dr. Juran flashed a smile, his teeth white against his dark skin. "That's my girl. All right, go out and check with the secretary, she'll schedule your evoked potentials. It will take a week or so to get you in," he warned. "So be patient."

"I will." This time would be easier as she really wasn't looking forward to the uncomfortable test anyway. After a few minutes the secretary fit her into the schedule for Tuesday the following week and Jillian gratefully returned to the ED.

She grabbed something quick to eat for lunch on her way past the cafeteria. She finished her sandwich in less than ten minutes and returned to the arena.

A familiar name on the whiteboard made her frown. Her burn patient, Mr. Perry, was still in his room. The dressing wouldn't have taken long so why was he still here? She went over to poke her head into his room.

"Mr. Perry, I'm surprised you're still here."

"It's my fault." Susan spoke up quickly. "I gave him his tetanus shot, then I was called away to help another nurse. Sorry. I'll get his dressing change done right away."

"It's OK." Mr. Perry waved his good hand. "I'm fine. Although I might take you up on that offer for pain medicine."

"Of course." Jillian glanced at Susan. "Why don't you give him a couple of percocets first?" She turned back to the patient as Susan went off to get the medicine. "Mr. Perry, I can't let you drive. You'll need to call someone to come and get you."

"I know." He sighed and pulled out his cellphone. Jillian jotted a few notes on his chart, listening while he explained to his ex-wife why he needed a ride. "She's not thrilled, but she's coming to get me," he said as he snapped his phone shut.

"Good." Jillian finished her notes, glanced at the clock and wrinkled her forehead. Everything was slow today. "I'll see what's taking Susan so long to get your medication."

"I'm not going anywhere," Mr. Perry said on a sigh.

Jillian pulled the curtain aside and crossed over to the

nurses' station. There were a group of people crowded around the medication dispensing machine.

"Susan? Did you get Mr. Perry's percocets?"

Susan disengaged herself from the gathering of nurses and shook her head. "I'm waiting for the pharmacy to send some."

Jillian tried not to snap but these delays were getting ridiculous. "Why? I thought the machine sent a message to pharmacy requesting a restock once the last dose was taken?"

"Yeah, but that's the problem." Susan's face was as red as her hair. "According to the inventory, there is supposed to be sixteen percocets left. But I didn't find any. They're missing."

Alec and his partner Rafe Hernandez were called out to the hospital moments after their evening shift started. He knew, even before Rose Jenkins had told him, that there must have been another diversion of narcotics.

After he and Rafe walked into the ED, they were met by the charge nurse, Luanne, who escorted them to a large conference room, her expression grave. "They're waiting inside."

Walking in, he scanned the faces in the room and found Jillian. Her face was pale and her smooth forehead was creased in a deep frown. He wanted to give her a reassuring smile, but he didn't.

He and Rafe took seats at the head of the table. Introductions were quickly made—Rose Jenkins, the nursing manager of the ED, Jillian Davis, the medical director of the unit, Margaret Strauss, Trinity's risk manager, and Dr. Chris Donnell, Chief of Staff. All of Trinity's leadership was present and accounted for.

"I need the list of all the staff members who were working during both narcotic thefts," Alec said.

Rose nodded and handed him a sheet of paper. "We've gathered the names, twenty-two in all, of those who were working during the timeframes in question. The first two nurses on the list have disciplinary action in their files— you might want to start with them. The five nurses with stars by their names were the ones who accessed the machine close to the timeframe of the diversion. On questioning them, several claimed they hadn't been to the machine, despite the computerized record, making us believe the thief is using staff passwords."

"The thefts also occurred during change of shift, a chaotic time when people are too busy to notice details," Jillian added, her face looking pale.

Damn. She looked as if she could use a hug.

"Is there no security camera over the narcotic dispensing machine?" Rafe asked.

"No. But in light of recent events, perhaps that's a step we will now be forced to take."

Hmm. Alec glanced at Rafe. Rather than a visible security camera that would possibly deter the thief, maybe a hidden camera could be placed to ensure they captured the culprit. He'd ask Rose Jenkins later about planting it. He didn't want anyone else to know it was there.

Jillian shifted in her seat, looking as if she wanted to say something but didn't.

Alec understood why she was upset. "I know it isn't easy, suspecting one of your own to be stealing narcotics, but if you could think about the people on this list and let me know if anyone has been acting different lately, we'd appreciate it."

Jillian's troubled gaze slid from his and he knew her name,

along with twenty-one others, was on the list. He didn't believe she was guilty—what could possibly be her motive? Yet he couldn't afford to ignore her as a suspect either.

"Is there anything else we can do to catch this person?" Rose asked.

He didn't have a good answer for her. "Is there a way to take all the percocets out of the machine?"

Rose and Jillian both looked horrified.

"No!" Rose exclaimed. "Our patients often need pain medication—we can't go without any narcotics."

"Besides," Jillian added, "if we lock them someplace else, the staff member could just as easily steal them from there. At least this way we have a record, even if it's not entirely accurate."

Yeah. Good point. All the more reason to install a hidden camera.

"We could ask for all these staff members to take a mandatory urine sample to test for drugs," Margaret, the risk manager, spoke up.

Rose shook her head. "No. I don't want to put the staff through that if we can avoid it."

"Besides, it's possible our suspect isn't taking the medication for themselves but for someone else." Jillian spoke up. "The drug tests would be inconclusive."

Alec jotted a few notes, agreeing with Jillian's point. The fact that Ricky had had percocets in his pocket meant that the drugs were being sold on the street. "Rafe and I would like to interview all the staff on this list."

"Good idea." Chris Donnell, who had been very quiet during the discussion, finally spoke up. "I expect you to let us know if you find anything."

Alec nodded. "Would you rather have me talk to the staff here at Trinity or down at the station?"

There was a long pause, before Rose said, "Down at the station might be better. That way, the rest of the staff won't know whose names are on the list. It's going to be tense enough around here until we find this person."

"All right. I'll take care of calling them and setting up the interviews." Alec took the list of staff suspects and folded it into his pocket. "Anything else you need from us?"

"No. We've instructed all staff members to change their passwords. We'll also continue to look for suspicious trends in accessing the narcotics. But thanks. We appreciate your help." Rose stood and Alec followed suit, rising to his feet as well.

He could feel Jillian's gaze on his back as he headed for the door. The leadership at Trinity must have respected her position as medical director to have included her in the meeting. Obviously, they didn't consider her a serious suspect. He glanced back, wishing there was a way to reassure her he believed in her innocence as well.

He tried to tell himself he believed she was innocent because of her integrity and the way she cared so much about her patients and not because he was physically attracted to her.

Giving his head a stern shake, he went out to his patrol car. No, at this point in the investigation, he didn't think his personal interest in Jillian would help her at all.

Jillian drove home, her stomach in knots as she tried not to think about her name being on the list of suspects.

Maybe she should go down and volunteer to be interviewed. Surely she'd feel better once she'd gotten that part over with. Would Alec interview her himself, or pass her along to his partner? And what difference did it make?

None. After sharing dinner with Alec and Shelby, she'd allowed herself the brief fantasy of thinking there could be something between them. But that had been before things had changed. Before there was another narcotic theft on her shift.

Alec had no choice but to view her as a suspect now. In fact, she was grateful Rose and Chris had allowed her to be a part of the meeting. She took her role as interim medical director seriously, would have loved to keep the position permanently.

She was innocent, she knew, but still it didn't look good to be linked as a suspect in the investigation. At least she felt better, knowing the hospital was working with the police. She trusted Alec's cool, logical brain would get to the bottom of the thefts.

The more she thought about it, the more she realized it would be better if she volunteered to have her interview with the police first, setting an example for the rest.

Cranking the steering-wheel, she maneuvered the car through a one-eighty degree turn and headed back to the freeway. Thanks to the rush-hour traffic, the trip to the third district police station took twice as long as it normally should.

When she pulled up in front of the police station, a flicker of doubt crept in. Was she making a mistake?

No. Squaring her shoulders, she gathered her courage and marched into the police station. When she asked to speak to officer Alec Monroe, she was politely told he was out on a call.

Of course he was. She should have known cops didn't

get jagged knife wounds from sitting behind a desk. She should have waited for him to contact her.

She turned away, ridiculously disappointed because she'd really wanted to get this over with. Not because of how she felt personally towards Alec, but because her career was at stake.

"Miss?"

She hesitated, glanced over her shoulder, and raised a brow. "Yes?"

"Would you wait for a few minutes? Officer Monroe just called in. He's on his way back to the precinct."

"Sure."

She sat down, gazing about with interest. Having never been inside a police station before, she was curious. The place didn't exactly look the way it was portrayed on TV.

When Alec walked in, her heart gave a betraying thump of awareness. When he flashed a smile that brightened his eyes, she sucked in a breath.

Oh, boy. Who was she kidding? This was definitely personal.

"Jillian," he greeted her warmly. "What brings you here?"

"I— Uh…" She hesitated, glancing around for his partner. "I thought it would be best to get my interview done right away. If you have time, that is."

His smile dimmed a bit and she couldn't help feeling her reason for being there had disappointed him. "I need Rafe to do your interview, since we've got to know each other on a personal basis."

"Yes, that makes sense." She swallowed, feeling awkward. "Is Rafe around? Or is he busy?"

Instead of answering her question, he stared at her for a long minute. His intense gaze made her all too aware of how impressive he looked in his blue uniform. He looked as if he wanted to say something, but didn't know how to say it.

"This is a bad time, isn't it?" She flashed a weak smile. "I'm sorry, Alec. I shouldn't have come unannounced. I'll wait to hear from you on the interview."

Before he could respond, a woman ran into the police station, crying hysterically. Alec protectively jumped in front of Jillian, facing the woman.

"Ma'am?" He put a hand out and the other hovered over his gun, anticipating an attack. "Calm down. Tell me what's wrong."

"My son is missing. You have to find my son." The woman was a wreck, sobbing and repeating herself over and over. Jillian couldn't blame her. She'd be out of control if her son was missing, too.

"OK, keep calm. We can help you." Alec stayed in front of Jillian. "All we need is a little more information."

The woman took a very deep breath, then her eyes rolled backward in her head as she crumpled to the floor.

She heard Alec mutter a curse under his breath as they both rushed over, each taking a place on either side of the woman's supine body.

"Do you have a pulse?" Jillian asked.

Alec shook his head. "I'll do compressions."

She nodded and pulled a resuscitation mouthpiece out of her purse. Ever since the first time she'd had to do mouth-to-mouth on a victim, she'd carried one for her own protection. After she gave the woman a quick breath, Alec went into compressions.

The officer behind the desk hurried over. "I already called for an ambulance. Is there anything else you need?"

"Do you have an automatic external defibrillator?"

"Nah, we don't have anything like that," the guy muttered, rubbing a hand over his bald head. "Stuff like this doesn't happen here."

Jillian stared down at the patient. The woman was young, in her late thirties. Too young to have had a heart attack.

Alec didn't seem to be listening, intent on his task. She kneeled across from him, watching and waiting for the right moment to give a breath.

"Excellent compressions, Alec. I feel a nice strong pulse."

He grinned and nodded, not interrupting his rhythm or his counting. She was impressed by how quickly he jumped into medical situations, as if he was a paramedic instead of a cop.

An ambulance siren shrilled loudly outside. In record time, Jillian thought. She stared down at the patient, giving the occasional breath and thinking the woman must have had some sort of underlying heart arrhythmia that had been exacerbated by stress. What else could have caused the abrupt change in her condition? Especially at her young age?

When the paramedics rushed through the door, Jillian gave orders. "Hook her up to the AED. She's going to need to be shocked."

Since she still wore her lab coat and name tag from work, they didn't question her authority. Within moments Alec stopped compressions just long enough for the electrodes to be placed.

The AED's mechanical voice rang out. "No pulse detected. Deliver a shock."

Jillian pushed the button herself, delivering the shock, and the woman's heartbeat returned on the screen. She reached for a pulse and felt one, thready but there.

"Get a couple of IVs in her and give a bolus of lidocaine. The way she went down, I suspect she has some underlying heart arrhythmia that went into V-fib as a result of her stress."

Alec went through the woman's purse, pulling out her driver's license as Jillian and the paramedics prepared the patient for transfer. When he caught her watching, he flushed.

"I'm sorry, but her son is missing. I have no choice but to go out and track down someone else who can give us the information we need."

"I understand." Of course Alec would be concerned about the missing boy. She understood. "Can I do anything to help?"

"No, but thanks." His smile was distracted.

"Hey, Monroe, that army medic training of yours has been coming in handy."

Jillian glanced at the officer behind the desk. Alec shrugged. "Thank the government. Your tax dollars paid for my training." He handed him the license. "Pull up this address for me, see if we have anything on this family."

So Alec had been trained as a medic. No wonder he was so good in the field. She helped the paramedics lift the woman onto their gurney. "I'm sure you guys can take it from here."

"You bet, Dr. Davis." One of the paramedics flashed a cocky grin as they wheeled the patient away.

She watched as Alec continued speaking in a low tone to the officer behind the desk. As she made her way toward the door, though, he caught up with her.

"Jillian, I have to run, but I'd like to talk later."

"Sure. I'll give you my pager number." She was about to rattle it off, but he shook his head.

"No need, I have it memorized. I'll call you," he said as they parted ways.

She lifted a hand to wave, but couldn't respond. Her insides had gone all soft and mushy, like a popsicle sitting in the sun on a hot summer day.

The idea that Alec had taken the time to memorize her pager number temporarily rendered her speechless.

CHAPTER FIVE

"DADDY?" A soft palm gently but insistently patted his cheek. "Daddy? Are you awake?"

Not exactly, but obviously his daughter was. Early mornings wouldn't have been a problem except for the fact he worked second shift. And last night he hadn't gotten home until much later than usual, well after midnight. Luckily, Meagan, the college girl he'd hired to stay with Shelby while he was working, didn't mind. Alec pried open one eye in a vain attempt to focus on his surroundings. The clock on his dresser read seven-thirty.

"Daddy, did you forget my birthday?"

What? He bolted upright from the bed, abruptly wide awake. He'd bought her a present, but had he wrapped it? Had he really forgotten? His mind frantically pinpointed the date. Tuesday. It was Tuesday, July fifteenth.

Shelby collapsed into a fit of giggles, making him realize he'd been had. The little minx. He scrunched his face into a mock frown. "Young lady, your birthday isn't until Saturday. Today is only Tuesday!"

"I got you, Daddy. You shoulda seen your face." She dissolved into another fit of giggles.

"Yeah, you got me," he agreed, a mischievous glint in his eye. "And do you know what that means?"

The giggles abruptly ceased. Shelby gasped and her beautiful brown eyes rounded comically. "What?"

"The Tickle Monster is going to get you." He gave her fair warning before he pounced. She shrieked, and the sound brought their dog Daisy, a white Westie terrier, galloping to the rescue. Alec kept his touch gentle, but tickled her belly until her giggles filled his head.

There was no better music than the sound of his daughter's laughter.

Daisy, their dog, jumped onto his bed and barked, sticking her nose between them as if trying to figure out how to join the fun as her tail wagged madly.

"Daddy, stop it!" she shouted between giggles. "You're making Daisy bark."

He nuzzled her neck, paused to press a kiss to her cute little nose and then threw himself back on the bed, his arms outstretched. He grimaced when Daisy licked his face. "He's gone. Daisy scared the Tickle Monster away."

Shelby climbed up to sit on his chest. Her shiny brown hair was tangled from their tussle and he reached up to smooth it back from her face, awestruck by how Shelby had somehow gotten the best of his and Liz's genes. "Are you going to take me and Daisy to the park this morning? You promised."

"Yep." He smiled when she patted his cheek again, apparently fascinated with his bristles. "I think you should probably let me shower and shave first."

She rolled her eyes. "That will take too long. Me and Daisy want to go *now*."

With a chuckle he nodded, unwilling to cause the light to dim in her eyes. What the heck, there was plenty of time for him to shave before the start of his shift. "All right. Let's eat something really fast for breakfast and then we'll go to the park."

"I already ate cereal," Shelby pointed out as he padded to the kitchen. He pursed his lips as he surveyed the room. Sure enough, there was a bowl surrounded by splashes of milk and other remnants of her breakfast stuck to the table.

Deciding the mess, too, could wait until later, he grabbed a cereal bar to tide him over before changing into a pair of cut-off shorts and his favorite T-shirt, the one Shelby had bought for his birthday, with Alaina's help, that read WORLD'S GREATEST DAD. Within ten minutes they were on their way outside, Shelby holding Daisy's leash as she skipped beside him.

The park was only a few short blocks from his house, one of the reasons he'd chosen the property in the first place. The minute he'd found out about Shelby, he hadn't wasted a second in preparing for her to live with him. He'd given up the lease on his bachelor apartment and found a small house in a nice neighborhood in record time. It had needed a bit of fixing up, but he'd worked on the repairs in his spare time. Luckily, his sister Alaina lived on the opposite side of the park, not too far away for the girls to get together for play dates.

His family had readily supported his decision to become a father for Shelby. He was grateful for all their help.

"One of the boys who splashed me hit his head on the bottom of the slide and blood gushed all over!" Shelby repeated the story from her adventure at the water park with relish. He shot her a wry look, wondering when his daughter had developed such a bloodthirsty streak. "Then a grown-up put a big white bandage over the bloody part until the ambulance came."

"Oh, yeah? I hope the cut didn't need stitches." He wondered if the child had been taken to Children's Memorial, located not far from Trinity Medical Center. The thought of Trinity reminded him of Jillian. Shelby continued to chatter but his attention wandered to the woman who haunted his dreams.

He hadn't been able to call Jillian. The hour had gotten so late last night he hadn't wanted to risk waking her. He glanced at his watch. He could possibly call her in a few hours, but he normally reserved his non-work daytime hours for Shelby. The very fact he was tempted to call Jillian anyway irked him.

His dreams of Jillian had been hot. Steamy hot. And he'd woken up in the middle of the night, hard and aching. Yet in the morning Shelby had been there, patting his cheek, forcing him to remember his priorities.

Shelby was the only woman he needed in his life. At least until she was eighteen and heading off to college. He was satisfied with the way things were.

He and Rafe had tracked down the missing boy, Kevin Sluzinski, just before midnight. Kevin and his best friend, Steve, had run away, intending to go stay at Steve's father's cabin on Pike Lake. They'd only gotten as far as Sheboygan, Wisconsin before getting tired and hungry. The story could have ended much worse, and as it was, telling Kevin about his mother's heart attack and subsequent hospitalization had been bad enough.

Throughout the search, a small part of him had been very grateful his own little girl had been safely home in bed. He couldn't imagine losing Shelby now that he'd found her.

A lithe woman was running along the sidewalk circling the park, heading toward them. For a moment he thought he was delusional because her features reminded him of Jillian. As she came closer, he realized the jogger really was Jillian. He smiled at her and her eyes widened with recognition.

At that moment, Daisy darted into her path.

"Daisy! No!" Shelby tugged sharply on the leash.

Jillian faltered, widening her step to avoid the dog, and he reacted instinctively, reaching out for her. He grabbed her arm, and the momentum caused her to fall against him with enough force to knock his breath away. He took two hasty steps back but managed to hold her upright.

He held her close, for a second or two longer than he should have, enjoying the silky feel of her skin against his and the exotic scent of her shampoo. Shelby continued to berate the dog as Jillian grasped his shoulders, shaking one foot to disentangle the leash.

"So sorry, Jillian," he said as she finally got free. "Are you all right?"

"Yes, I think so." Her voice was breathless, her face red from exertion. Having Jillian in his arms was pure heaven. He'd wanted to pull her close for a kiss the night he'd walked her to her car at the lakefront, but he hadn't dared touch her, especially in front of Shelby. As if sensing his thoughts, her eyes widened and focused momentarily on his mouth before she turned to look at Shelby, who was crouched beside Daisy. "Hello again, Shelby. How are you?"

"Fine." Shelby's face was contrite as the dog barked at

her feet. "This is my dog Daisy. She didn't mean to trip you, honest!"

"Of course she didn't," Jillian agreed. Reluctantly, Alec allowed her to extricate herself from his embrace so she could reach down to pet Daisy, whose fluffy white body was wiggling with excitement. "She's adorable."

Alec wasn't sure if Jillian was referring to his daughter or the dog, but noticed how she winced a little when she put her full weight on her foot. He reached for her again, taking her arm. "Easy, I think you've twisted your ankle."

"I'm sure I'll be fine," Jillian assured him, reaching down to give it a rub. "I stepped funny, but it wasn't bad."

"Here, there's a park bench just a few feet away." He wrapped a supporting arm around her waist. "Let's have you sit down for a minute."

"I'm fine," she protested, but limped over to the bench. Once they were both seated, she wiped her forearm across her brow. "I didn't realize you and Shelby lived around here, Alec."

He could have said the same. He hadn't realized Jillian lived so close to him either. And now that he did know, he thought the park might be his favorite place to walk in the mornings. "I have a house over on Union Avenue."

"My bee sting is all better, see?" Shelby blurted, holding up her arm.

"Shelby, it's not polite to interrupt," Alec scolded lightly.

"I do see." Jillian leaned forward, smiling as she examined the spot on Shelby's arm. "I'm glad you're better."

"Did you really put stitches in my daddy?" Shelby asked.

Alec frowned, wondering what had made Shelby remember that. After they'd left Jillian on Sunday evening, he'd explained to his daughter how he'd met Jillian at the hospital when she'd taken care of him, although he'd been careful not to let Shelby know the wound had been from a knife.

"Yes, I did." Jillian nodded solemnly. "He was very brave, just like you."

Shelby seemed pleased, climbing up on the bench beside her. "Guess what? I'm gonna be a doctor when I grow up, too."

"Really?" Alec and Jillian said at the same time. Jillian laughed and Alec glanced at her, wishing he had taken the time to shower and shave before running into her. Literally. Of course, then again, if he had, their paths might not have crossed at all.

Better to be scruffy, he decided.

He turned his attention to Shelby. "No wonder you were so interested in the boy who bled all over the water park," he commented in a dry tone.

Jillian raised a brow at his comment. "Hmm. Well, Shelby, if you really want to be a doctor, you have to study really hard in school. Do you like school?" She leaned down to rub her ankle again and Daisy licked her fingers as if to say she was sorry.

"Yes. School is fun," Shelby announced. "I have lots of friends there. They're all coming to my birthday party this Saturday. Will you come, too?"

"Oh, I…uh…I don't know…" Jillian's gaze cut to Alec's in panic.

"That's a great idea," he agreed, ignoring the way Jillian's eyes took on an exasperated expression. She wasn't high on the list of suspects. Once Rafe did the interview, there was no reason they couldn't get together as friends at his daughter's party. "There will be at least a dozen six- and seven-year-olds there and I could use all the help I can get." His family planned to help, but he liked the idea of having Jillian over, too.

"Please?" His daughter turned big, pleading eyes toward Jillian. "Then for sure Daisy will know you're not mad at her."

"I'll stop by if I'm not working," Jillian hedged. "And Daisy already knows I'm not mad at her. Look, she's trying to untie my running shoes."

Shelby giggled when the dog took a shoelace between her teeth and tugged. Just that quickly the crisis was over and Shelby launched onto another topic, something other than her impending birthday party. Alec knew Jillian had wanted to refuse. Was she working or had it been an excuse?

He should have felt guilty for backing her into a corner, but he didn't. There was nothing wrong with being friends, right? Jillian gave him the impression of being a loner and he'd learned the value of family and friends over this past year.

"We'll walk you home," Alec said when Jillian stood and tested her weight on her ankle.

"There's no need, see?" Jillian lifted her foot and rotated the joint, proving it was fine. "It's really not painful at all."

"We'll walk you home, anyway," he repeated, refusing to take no for an answer.

They strolled along the sidewalk surrounding the park. He kept pace with Jillian while Shelby ran ahead with Daisy, running in circles on the grass.

"She's beautiful." This time, he knew she meant Shelby.

"Thanks." His throat closed with pent up emotion. "I

feel bad I wasn't there for her early years, but I cherish every moment I have with her now."

Jillian sent him a sidelong glance. "I know it's not my business, but why didn't you know about her?"

It was a fair question. His family had wondered the exact same thing. "Her mother and I were together for about a year but things didn't work out. We were just too different. Honestly, I don't think I was quite ready to settle down, even though it was Liz who broke things off."

"But she was pregnant." Jillian frowned.

"She couldn't have known at the time, based on Shelby's birthday. And I certainly didn't know." He couldn't help the defensive note in his voice. He didn't like anyone assuming he'd abandoned his responsibilities. "There's no way I would have left if I'd known about Shelby. We used precautions. Apparently Liz managed to get pregnant while taking birth-control pills."

"She never contacted you?" Jillian pressed.

He shook his head. Heck, he must have asked himself the same question a dozen times. Why hadn't Liz called him? Why hadn't she told him about the baby? He didn't understand, yet she wasn't here to ask. "No, in fact, I'd heard she moved to Florida. I'm not sure why she didn't tell me. Toward the end, things were strained between us, but I'm sure she could have used financial support." It bothered him, to think about Liz taking the burden of raising a child alone.

"I can imagine," Jillian murmured. Their fingers brushed, clung for a minute, before she pulled away.

He told himself to finish the story. "It wasn't until a year ago that I got the call from the department of health and human services. They contacted me because Liz had listed me as the father on Shelby's birth certificate. Liz had cervical cancer and before she died she gave instructions, requesting Shelby be placed with me."

Jillian raised a brow. "Did you have DNA testing? To make sure she's yours?"

"No need." He followed Shelby and Daisy with his gaze as they ran through the park. His tone was firm. "She's mine."

He waited for Jillian to argue—he'd heard it all from his siblings and parents. They'd really wanted him to get DNA tests too, but to his surprise, Jillian didn't push the issue.

"Poor Shelby." Jillian gazed out at his daughter with a frown furrowing in her brow. "I imagine it must have been hard for her, living with a stranger after her mother died."

He paused at the corner of the park, waiting for Shelby and Daisy to catch up. "Yeah, it was a little rough, but we made it. My family helped. A lot." He truly owed his family a debt of gratitude. "Between us, we surrounded her with love. And, as I mentioned, kids are resilient."

"Shelby is lucky to have you. Your family sounds great," she agreed. Jillian smiled and dropped the subject as Shelby and Daisy ran up. "This is the road I live on, Ranger Road."

"Ranger Road?" Shelby echoed, skipping with Daisy at her heels. "Like the Power Rangers?"

"Not exactly. Here, take my hand as we cross the street," Alec warned, reaching for her. Shelby took his hand and the three of them and the dog crossed over. Alec was conscious of how much they probably looked like the typical happy family.

The thought gave him pause. Family was great, but his past experience with relationships had been anything but stellar. The way Liz had disappeared from his life was proof of that.

Within a few minutes they'd reached Jillian's house. He was pleased to note hers was very similar to his, a cute little Cape Cod.

"This is it," Jillian said, slowing her step. "Thanks for seeing me home."

"Our pleasure, right, squirt?" He glanced at Shelby.

"Right." His daughter nodded. "Don't forget my birthday party, Dr. Jillian. Saturday at three."

Alec wished his verbose daughter would shut up about the party, but Jillian only laughed. "I'll check my schedule," she told Shelby.

"That's enough," he reminded his daughter. "Say goodbye."

"Goodbye, Dr. Jillian."

"It was nice meeting you again, Shelby." When Jillian glanced at him, he resisted the urge to haul her into his arms to kiss her. "I'll, uh, call you later." He cleared his throat, hating the moment of awkwardness. "We…uh, Rafe and I will be in touch. About the interview."

"I understand. I'll be around all day," Jillian offered.

Shelby tugged on his arm, reminding him that he didn't have free time that afternoon. Or any time soon. With regret, he shook his head. "I don't have free time this afternoon."

"Are you working second shift tonight?" Jillian asked.

"Yeah. You, too?" He brightened at the prospect.

She nodded. "I start at three."

So did he. Figured, their work schedules happened to be one of the few things between them that matched. He couldn't quite find the humor in that thought.

"All right, we'll try and get in touch with you tonight—if we're not too busy," he cautioned. "If we're slammed with calls, we won't make it." If there were too many calls for violent crimes, interviewing Jillian would have to fall to the bottom of his priority list.

"I understand," she answered easily, not seeming nearly as upset about not seeing him as he'd like her to be. She turned to walk toward the driveway leading up to her house. "Bye, Alec."

"Bye." He watched her walk away, wishing desperately that he could follow, to talk to her some more—and not necessarily about the percocet case. Despite how Shelby continued to tug on his arm, he didn't move, not an inch, until Jillian had disappeared into her house.

"Come on, Daddy. You said we were going to the park!"

"I'm coming, I'm coming." Reluctantly, he turned and began walking back the way they'd come.

"I like Dr. Jillian, Daddy. She's nice."

"Yes, she is." Alec stared down at his daughter, grinning as she jumped and skipped over the cracks in the sidewalk, making a game of things. Fantasizing over Jillian wasn't smart. He didn't have a lot of spare time on his hands or room in his life for a relationship.

It struck him that a woman like Jillian deserved much more than being relegated to the bottom of his priority list.

CHAPTER SIX

JILLIAN didn't see Alec that night, or the one after that. Rafe had called for an interview but she'd been disappointed Alec hadn't been anywhere around.

On Thursday she gave herself a stern lecture. It was time to stop acting like an adolescent schoolgirl, waiting for Alec to ask her to the prom. So what if he hadn't made the time to come and see her. The man certainly had his hands full between his career as a police officer and being a single dad.

If only she hadn't run into him at the park. Seeing him in his casual jeans and T-shirt, his cheeks darkened by early morning stubble, grinning at his daughter, had been enough to make her imagine what it would be like to snuggle up in bed with him. She could easily see them greeting their daughter as they started the day.

The image was so clear she caught her breath. Fantasy was one thing, but none of her previous relationships with men had prepared her for Alec. Every time he was near, she longed for his touch. She couldn't think straight around him.

Jillian gave her head a quick shake. Enough foolishness. All through medical school she'd been focused on her goal of becoming a doctor. Her parents had sacrificed a portion of their retirement fund to finance her education. Graduating at the top of her class had made her mother proud.

Some of her female counterparts had lamented the long hours required of the residency program, claiming their biological clocks were ticking away. She'd never fully understood the yearning they'd felt, not even when she'd done her OB rotation.

Until now.

She couldn't deny the very tangible connection she felt with Shelby, especially when the little girl had leaned against her so trustingly. They had a lot in common. They'd both lost their mothers, and they both cared about Alec.

"Jillian?"

She roused herself from her thoughts and turned to see Dr. Chris Donnell, the chief of staff, approaching. Instinctively she straightened her spine.

"Good evening, Chris. How are you?"

Her boss didn't smile. In fact, his brows were pulled together in a frown. He glanced around and then gently pulled her to a quiet area to talk. Her stomach clenched in warning.

"Do you have any idea who is stealing these narcotics?"

She frowned. "No. If I did, I'd tell the police."

Chris pursed his lips. "I don't need to tell you, this situation is very disturbing. Anything you can do to find the guilty party and resolve this issue is of utmost importance."

She swallowed hard at his stern tone. "Yes, I completely agree."

He rocked back on his heels. "I hope I haven't made a mistake in naming you as the interim medical director, Jillian. I need a true leader in this position."

Her face burned at the implied reprimand, but she forced a confident tone. "We'll find the guilty person. Granting me this position wasn't a mistake." She'd learned early on the best way to get ahead in a male-dominated profession was to ooze confidence while touting your abilities. "I'm the right person for this role. I'm sure we'll get this situation under control soon."

Her boss gave a brief nod. "I hope you're right. I've had a private meeting with the police on this very issue. They've scheduled an appointment to review how the narcotic dispensing device works. Please, give them your assistance."

"Of course." Alec was here? Where? She glanced around the arena, and then spotted him standing off to one side next to Rafe. She crossed over, greeting them both, but a warm glow burned in her belly when Alec's gaze lingered on hers in a special, silent greeting.

"I thought maybe you guys had already gotten a demo on this machine," Jillian said.

"No, things have been crazy." He waved a hand. "Do you mind showing us how it works?"

She went through the mechanics of the dispensing machine, although the numbness and tingling in her fingers, curiously absent over the past few days, had returned. She'd kept her routine of running three miles every other morning and so far she hadn't noticed anything different. The five percent chance of still having MS or some other auto-immune disorder seemed more and more like a figment of her imagination.

"Jillian, there's a victim of a motor vehicle crash coming in," Luanne informed her as she finished the demonstration.

Jillian glanced down at her pager with a frown. "Oh? Why didn't we get a trauma call?"

At that moment, her pager went off. She raised a brow.

"We're having some trouble with our paging system," Luanne explained. "Don't worry, someone's here, looking at the system."

"Good to know. Thanks, Lu." Jillian read the message on the display. "Fifty-two-year-old white male being admitted with blunt trauma to the chest and head. Vitals stable." Didn't sound too bad, for a trauma call.

"We're putting him in trauma bay one." Luanne wrote the description up on the whiteboard. "If he's fairly stable, we can always move him into the arena."

"All right. If you need anything else in the meantime, let me know." Jillian glanced back toward Rafe and Alec. "I'm sorry, but I need to get back to work. Is there anything else you need?"

"Just a quick question." Alec frowned. "I noticed you used a password to get into the machine. I could see what you entered from right behind you."

She flushed. "Yes, it's not the most foolproof system in the world. All we can do is recommend all staff change their passwords if they think someone else may have seen it."

"Right." He and Rafe exchanged a glance. "I think we'll hang around for a while, if you don't mind."

She smiled. "Of course I don't mind."

Within minutes she heard the doors to the ambulance bay open, announcing the arrival of their blunt trauma patient. Jillian hurried over to the first trauma bay.

"Vital signs are good, although his blood pressure is on the high side, not sure what his baseline is," the paramedic announced. "Glasgow coma score of 20, responding to verbal commands. Eighteen-gauge left peripheral IV placed in the field, 500 ccs of normal saline infused."

Will Patterson, the ED nurse in the trauma room, connected the patient to the heart monitor.

Jillian glanced at the patient's ambulance paperwork, read his name as Barry Cox and approached his bedside. She leaned over the gurney in an attempt to examine him. Barry was an extremely large man with a long bloody gash across his forehead. A strong odor of alcohol emanated from him, which she tried to ignore as she assessed his neuro status for herself. "Mr. Cox? Can you open your eyes for me?"

Barry Cox opened his eyes, saw her leaning close and suddenly went wild. She reared backward when he sat upright on the gurney, the abrupt movement yanking his IV out of his left arm. The heart leads Will had connected landed on the floor.

"I'll get you for this!" Barry shouted, swinging his arm toward Jillian with the intention of hitting her. "I'll get you!"

She tried to duck from the blow, but his fist hit her right shoulder, causing a sharp pain to zing down her arm. Before she realized what was happening, Alec was there, putting himself between her and the wild patient.

"Mr. Cox, you'd better sit down," Alec advised in a calm tone, although his eyes flashed with a glint of anger. Will, the paramedics and Alec tried to surround the patient, but they couldn't get too close. "The staff here want to help you, but not if you're going to fight against them."

"I don't need any help!" Barry was full of false bravado, even as he swayed on his feet. Jillian suspected his head and his chest, both of which had hit the steering-wheel, hurt like the devil. Or maybe he didn't feel any pain through the alcohol haze. "Leave me alone!"

Jillian tried to step around Alec, but he frowned and moved so his body remained between her and Barry. She stifled a sigh and captured Barry's gaze, imploring him to listen. "Mr. Cox, please, sit down. I need to make sure you don't have a head injury or any cracked ribs. Does your chest hurt?"

As if on cue, Barry rubbed the center of his chest. "Yeah, hurts a little."

She edged around Alec, who kept his gaze trained on the patient. "Mr. Cox, my name is Dr. Davis. I'd really like to examine you. What if you have other injuries?"

"I'm fine." He took a step backward and Alec followed. Barry frantically searched for the door. "I just want to go home."

Boy, he was stubborn. "Mr. Cox, you can't go home until you let me examine you."

"I can go home if I say I'm going home." Barry took another step in the general direction of the door. "You can't stop me. I have rights."

"You do have rights, but I think we need to make sure your head injury isn't clouding your judgment." As much as she wanted to let Barry walk out the door, she was liable for his care. She couldn't let him go until she saw the CT scan of his head. If the scan was negative, she'd be more than happy to discharge him. "Why don't you just co-operate with us? Once we make sure your head is fine, I'll allow you to go home."

For a moment she thought she had him, but he turned

and bolted for the door. Alec and the paramedics went after him and between them wrestled him to the floor.

"Give him 5 milligrams of Haldol IM so we can get his IV replaced," Jillian ordered. Will dashed over to get the medication.

Barry continued to struggle as Alec and the paramedics held him down. Once Will had given the sedative, Jillian knelt beside Alec. "Whenever you're ready, we can lift him back onto the gurney."

"We'll lift him—just get out of the way."

Startled by Alec's abrupt tone, she backed off and the three men lifted the heavy patient back onto the gurney. They continued to hold Barry's extremities while she placed another antecubital IV.

When Barry began to struggle again, she shook her head. "I'll have to intubate him and give major sedation just to get a CT scan of his head."

"Here's the airway box," Will spoke up, setting the intubation supplies on her right.

She could feel Alec's gaze on her as she prepared to intubate the patient. Holding the laryngoscope in her right hand wasn't easy and she prayed her fingers wouldn't go numb as she lifted the jaw enough to visualize the airway. Just as she slid the endotracheal tube into his larynx, the laryngoscope slipped. She muttered a curse under her breath as she advanced the tube blindly, praying the tube was in the correct place. "Where's respiratory therapy? I need someone to check this tube placement."

The RT whose name-tag read Mike placed a small device on the end of the endotracheal tube, "Placement looks good."

Jillian wasn't convinced and reached for her stetho-scope. "Mike, hold this tube secure, I want to listen." When she heard breath sounds in both lungs, overwhelming relief made her knees weak. Her numbness and tingling hadn't hurt the patient, thank heavens. She nodded at Will. "It's in. Give him ten milligrams of Versed."

Will had the medication ready and soon every muscle in Barry Cox's body relaxed. Alec and the paramedics were finally able to let go.

"Whew. Thanks, everyone." Jillian glanced around to find the nurse. "Will, call over to Radiology, let them know we need a stat CT of the head."

"Consider it done." Will grabbed the nearest phone. Luanne came over with wrist and ankle restraints, in case the Versed didn't hold Barry for long.

Jillian helped place the restraints on Barry's wrists and ankles. Will hung up the phone. "They're ready for him now."

"Good." Jillian stepped back. "I hope he sleeps like a baby the entire time."

"Me, too," Will commented in a dry tone and he and the respiratory therapist got in position to push the gurney. Jillian offered a wan smile as they wheeled Barry away.

She lifted a hand to rub the area where Barry's fist had connected with her shoulder.

"Are you OK?" Alec asked in a low tone. "Why on earth didn't you get out of the way?"

She quickly understood his irritation had more to do with the situation than with her personally. She shouldn't have been relieved but she was. "I'm fine. I just need to get some ibuprofen. Thanks for all your help, Alec. Excuse me," she added, turning to head back to her office. She needed a moment alone and, besides, there was a stash of ibuprofen somewhere in her desk, she was certain.

Alec followed. "Jillian, maybe you should call one of the orthopedic surgeons down to take a look at your arm."

She found the ibuprofen and dropped three into the palm of her hand, which still held a slight tremor from the near assault. She tossed them back with some water from a half-finished water bottle on her desk. The physical altercation with Barry Cox had jarred her more than she wanted to admit. "It's just a muscle ache, he didn't hit me very hard."

Alec scowled. "Looked hard enough from where I was standing. And I noticed your hand was affected—you almost dropped the laryngoscope. I'm worried about you."

The close call with the laryngoscope had been too much. What if she'd harmed the patient? She flexed her fingers and abruptly sat down behind her desk. After the emotionally draining situation, she didn't have the energy to lie. Better he knew the truth anyway. "The problem with my hand isn't related to my shoulder."

Alec crossed over, pushed a pile of her paperwork aside so he could sit on the edge of her desk, facing her. "What is the problem, then?"

He was close, too close, and the need to seek refuge in his arms was too strong. Tears burned her eyes but she blinked them away. "I don't know. My neurologist can't seem to find a diagnosis. But it might be serious."

"Neurologist?" Alec reached over and took one of Jillian's hands in his. "Has he ordered testing?"

Alec's hands felt so warm and strong around hers. She stared at their entwined fingers for a moment. Then took a deep breath and nodded. "I'm going next Tuesday for evoked potentials." At his confused expression, she went on to explain, "It's a painful test where they poke needles into my nerves in order to measure the response."

"Ouch," Alec muttered. He drew her up to her feet, urging her close. "Jillian, I'm sorry. If there's anything I can do…"

"There isn't." But it was sweet of him to ask. He continued to pull her closer until she was wrapped in his arms in a secure hug.

Giving in to the need to be held, she briefly rested her head on his shoulder. For a moment she savored being able to lean on someone strong. He stroked a hand down her back and she wished she could stay like that for the rest of the night. But she couldn't. In fact, another patient could come in any second.

With real regret Jillian lifted her head and glanced up at Alec, intending to thank him. Before her lips could form the words, he dipped his head and captured her mouth with his.

He tasted like cinnamon and a hint of coffee. She parted her lips, seeking more. He took her invitation and deepened the kiss. Seconds extended into long minutes as the kiss changed from something sweet to something needy. Edgy. Hungry.

In some distant part of her brain she knew he meant to offer comfort, but there wasn't anything simple about the way their mouths fused as one. Suddenly she couldn't get enough, tugging on his broad shoulders, urging him closer.

He widened his stance to bring her up against his hard length. As his body cradled hers, a thrill shuddered down her spine.

Her pager went off with a shrill beep. For a moment she was seriously tempted to ignore it, but she didn't. Breaking away from Alec, breathing heavily, she groped for the device. With an effort, she focused her gaze on the readout, barely able to see through the red haze of desire.

"They must have fixed the paging system. I have another patient coming in," she told him unnecessarily. "A woman with belly pain."

"How long?" His voice was low, gravelly.

"A few minutes." She stepped back, not that there was a whole lot of room between her desk and the wall. "I, uh, have to go."

He nodded, running a hand through his hair. "Jillian, do you work on Saturday?"

"No." At first she thought he was going to ask her out, and then belatedly remembered his daughter's party. "Alec, I don't think—"

"Shelby's been asking about you," he confessed. "You're her hero after the bee sting. She keeps talking about wanting to be a doctor, just like you. Would you please come, even for a short time? It would mean a lot to her."

And to him? The unspoken question was there between them. She knew going to his house, to his daughter's birthday party, was treading on dangerous ground. But right now, with her lips tingling from his kiss, and her body longing to be molded against his, she couldn't refuse. Especially because she didn't want to disappoint Shelby. "I'd love to come. Three o'clock, right?"

His lips curved in a grin. "Right." He turned and plucked a pen from her desk and scribbled his address and phone number on a scrap of paper. "Here. Call me if something comes up and you can't make it. I'll explain to Shelby that your ability to come depends on work."

Clearly, Alec would do anything to protect his daughter, even if that meant making up an excuse on her behalf. Rather than being annoyed by the knowledge, she was touched by his concern. Did he really expect her to renege on the party? She'd had her doubts about going, sure, but she wouldn't deliberately lie to him. Or to his daughter. "Nothing, except maybe a busload of trauma patients, would prevent me from coming to Shelby's birthday." She placed a reassuring hand on his arm. "I promise."

She didn't make promises lightly. The way he held her gaze told her he realized that. He took her hand and brushed a quick kiss along her knuckles. She sucked in a quick breath, very sensitive to the firmness of his lips against her fingers. Alec made the simple gesture gallant. "Thanks. I can't wait to see you again."

The husky words sent a shaft of longing radiating down her spine. "Me, too," she whispered.

CHAPTER SEVEN

ALEC found himself anxiously waiting with less patience than Shelby for the day of her party to arrive.

For one thing, he'd be glad when his job of hosting dozens of six- and seven-year-olds was over. He wanted everything to go off without a hitch for Shelby's sake. His daughter deserved a memorable celebration for her seventh birthday.

But he couldn't lie to himself. The main reason he was looking forward to Saturday was because he wanted desperately to see Jillian again.

He hadn't been able to erase the taste of her from his mind. If anything, he intended to kiss her again. Soon. During that short time in her office, he'd completely forgotten where they'd been. Until her darned pager had gone off.

Remaining celibate for the past year hadn't been difficult. From the moment he'd found out about Shelby, he'd been single-minded in his goal to create a home for his daughter. Women and dating hadn't been a part of his grand plan.

Only now, after the electrifying kiss he'd shared with Jillian, his body reminded him just how long he'd been without a woman.

Very long. Too long.

He shook his head. If he had half a brain, he'd go find some one-night stand to get sex out of his system. Except for one tiny problem. He wasn't the least bit interested in a one-night stand.

All of his desires seemed to be focused on one woman. Jillian.

He hadn't intended to get caught up in a relationship but, after kissing Jillian, he couldn't deny they were headed in that direction. Was he nuts to pursue Jillian? Shelby needed to be his primary concern. His daughter had been through the most difficult transition he could imagine, losing her mother to cancer and then moving a thousand miles away to live with a father she didn't know. Upsetting the peaceful balance they'd found over the past eight months wasn't an option.

Friends. Yeah, that was the way to handle this. Concentrate on being friends. Which meant no more kissing. Jillian certainly could use a friend right now. In her office last night, she'd seemed so lonely. No one should have to worry about a painful test all alone.

He wished he could talk to her about the percocet case, but he couldn't. He and Rafe had interviewed dozens of kids on the Barclay Park football team, but no one would talk to them. Every single kid denied having seen Ricky, the boy who'd been shot, with any percocets in his possession.

Rafe thought he was nuts, looking for a connection between football players and percocets, but he couldn't help thinking the two were somehow related. Heck, he'd played football in high school and the morning after a tough game his entire body had hurt.

Maybe it was a stretch, but it was the only theory he could come up with at the moment.

Daisy began barking like a mad dog, diverting his attention to the impending party. Shelby ran into the kitchen to get him.

"Daddy, the giant blow-up games are here!"

"I'm coming." Setting aside his coffee, he allowed Shelby to drag him outside. Sure enough, the inflatable slide and mini-trampoline were being assembled in his back yard.

Shelby hopped from one foot to the other. "Can I try them out before my friends get here? Please?"

"Honey, it's going to take these guys at least an hour to get them inflated with air. Come inside for now and we'll try out your games later."

Dejected, Shelby went back inside the house. Alec spent a few minutes making sure the people setting up the play equipment had everything they needed before he walked back inside, too.

In the kitchen, he finished his coffee, and then went through his mental check list. Pizza? Check. Cake? Check. Ice cream? Check. Goodie-bags? Check. Balloons? Check. What on earth was he forgetting? Oh, yeah, juice boxes. Check.

He took a deep breath. Everything was ready to go. All he needed was to shower and get dressed. In less than an hour, his family would descend upon him.

And despite his internal let's-be-friends speech, he was more than a little curious to see how well Jillian got along with his family.

His family was early. Bless their hearts, his sisters, Alaina and Abby, were worried he wouldn't have things under control.

For once he showed them he was capable of being a good father. Or at the very least a responsible one.

He didn't mind when they helped him clean up his house, even though he knew darned well the place would be trashed by the time Shelby's friends left. His family's efforts since he'd taken custody of Shelby were very much appreciated.

One by one Shelby's guests arrived. Each of the parents promised to return in four hours, at seven o'clock that evening to pick up their little darlings. As several of the girls shrieked, making Daisy bark, Alec prayed he'd last that long.

Once all the girls were present and accounted for, Alec and his brother Adam supervised the kids as they played on the inflatable slide and trampoline. He didn't even notice when Jillian arrived, until Alaina came out to replace him.

"Better go and chat with your friend," Alaina said with a nod in Jillian's direction. "She looks a little shell-shocked over there."

"Thanks." Alec didn't need to be asked twice. As he approached he heard Abby giving Jillian a brief history on every member of the entire Monroe family.

"Adam is a pediatrician, you'll have a lot in common with him. Alaina, she used to be a nurse, but she quit her job after she had Beth because her husband Scott travels too much for her to work a set schedule. Austin has just returned home after completing his residency in St. Louis." Abby flashed Alec a wide, cheeky grin when she saw him. "Oh, hi, Alec. I was just trying to help Jillian put names to faces."

"Abby, I think you've overwhelmed her." He noticed Jillian clutched a large gift-wrapped box, her eyes wide as she took in the adults scattered among the girls. "Hey, don't worry," he quickly assured her. "You already met Adam, right? Austin isn't here, so that's one less family member to worry about. I promise there's no test on the names."

"To think I used to ace tests." Jillian shook her head and gave a faint smile. "Hi, Alec." Jillian thrust a large box into his hands. "This is for Shelby."

"Great. Come on in, I do have a few adult drinks to offer, you won't be forced to pick from the selection of juice boxes."

They headed into the house, Abby following hot on their heels. Jillian glanced around, seemingly curious to see how he lived. He mentally thanked his sister's cleaning efforts.

"So, Jillian, how long have you known my brother the cop?" Abby didn't seem to realize she was being incredibly nosy.

"A few months," Jillian admitted. "I stitched up his knife wound when he came to the ED."

He hid a wince as he placed Jillian's gift amongst the others in the corner of the living room.

"Knife wound?" Abby swung around to pin him with a narrow gaze. "And why didn't I hear anything about a knife wound?"

"Why do you think?" he countered. Ignoring his younger sister, he turned to Jillian. "What would you like to drink? Coffee? Water? Beer? Wine?"

"I think I'll stick with water for now." Jillian definitely looked uncomfortable.

"Relax, I swear my family is harmless," he told her under his breath as he handed her a bottle of water.

"Maybe, but I didn't realize there'd be so many of them."

He grimaced. "I know. All our names starting with the

letter *A* doesn't help." He lifted up a hand. "And don't say it, we've heard all the A-team jokes known to man."

She laughed and he relaxed a bit, taking her back outside to meet his parents. He made the introductions but there wasn't time for more questions because when Shelby caught sight of Jillian she ran over.

"Hi, Dr. Jillian!" Shelby threw her arms around Jillian's waist for a quick hug. "Thanks for coming to my party."

"Thanks for inviting me." Jillian returned Shelby's hug and Alec was struck by how natural they looked together. Jillian glanced over to where the kids were taking turns going down the inflatable slide. "Looks like you're having fun, Shelby."

"Lots of fun. My dad is the best dad in the whole world!" Shelby broke away from Jillian to treat him to an exuberant hug before running back over to join her friends.

Alec half expected Jillian to take off after the first hour, but she hung in there through the games, the pizza, the cake and ice cream and finally the gifts. When Shelby sat down to open her presents, she went to Jillian's gift first.

"A doctor's bag!" Alec's jaw dropped when Shelby opened up a doctor's kit, nothing like the plastic ones you got in the stores. Jillian had put together a real bag full of actual instruments and supplies—all child-friendly, of course. "I love it, Dr. Jillian. Thanks so much!"

"You're welcome." Jillian blushed as almost every Monroe stared at her, as if gauging how close Jillian was to becoming a permanent member of the family.

He stifled a sigh. His family meant well, but Jillian wasn't vying to be Shelby's stepmother.

Was she?

No. She was simply a generous person. He figured the main reason Jillian had come was because she hadn't wanted to disappoint Shelby. Turning his attention to his daughter, he watched as she went through the rest of her presents. There was still time after the gift opening before parents started picking up their kids, so he shooed the girls back outside. Shelby carefully carried her precious gifts into her room.

He went outside to keep an eye on the girls. He stood by the slide, waiting for Shelby to return. When she didn't come back outside right away, he left Adam in charge and headed back into the house.

Walking down the hall towards Shelby's room, he heard voices. Slowing his steps, he shamelessly eavesdropped.

"My mommy died of cancer," Shelby was saying in a matter-of-fact tone. "And the doctors tried to save her life, but they couldn't. I think by the time I'm a grown-up, doctors will know how to cure cancer, don't you?"

"Yes, I do." Jillian's voice was soft. "I think you're a very brave girl to want to help others, Shelby."

"When I first came here I cried a lot because I missed my mommy," Shelby confessed. "But now I have my daddy, and my grandma and grandpa, and all my aunts and uncles. A whole family of my own."

"You have a wonderful family," Jillian murmured.

"Yes, I know. Especially my daddy. I love him best of all. Do you like my daddy, Dr. Jillian?"

There was a long pause and Alec held his breath, waiting for Jillian's answer.

"Of course I like your daddy. He's a very nice man."

"Good. Because I think he likes you, too."

Whoa, what was this? His seven-year-old daughter was

arranging his love life? Deciding he'd eavesdropped long enough, he rapped on the doorframe a moment before entering Shelby's room, finding both Shelby and Jillian sitting cross-legged on the floor.

"There you are, Shelby. Your friends are all outside. You should go and say your goodbyes because their parents will be coming to pick them up any minute."

"OK, Daddy." Shelby jumped to her feet. He gave Jillian a hand to help her up. "Thanks again for coming to my party." Shelby gave Jillian another quick hug before dashing outside to join her friends.

"What was that all about?" he asked, as if he hadn't overheard a good portion of their conversation.

Jillian's gaze was serious. "Nothing really. A little girl-talk, that's all."

He told himself not to push his luck and satisfied himself with tucking a strand of Jillian's hair behind her ear. "I want you to know how much I appreciate you coming today. Your presence meant a lot to Shelby." After a moment's hesitation, he added, "And to me. You have no idea how terrifying a dozen young girls can be."

Jillian laughed. "If you think they're terrifying now, wait until they're sixteen and getting ready to go to the prom."

The image of Shelby in a slinky dress with her hair piled on her head made him wince. He put a hand to his chest. "Don't. Please. I can't go there yet."

Her smile was surprisingly sad. "I think you're going to do just fine."

She moved to step past him, to leave Shelby's room, but he caught her hand in his. "Jillian, what's wrong?"

"Nothing is wrong, Alec." Was it his imagination or

was her bright smile a bit forced? "Come on, you'd better be there to say goodbye to your daughter's guests."

She was right, so he reluctantly dropped the subject, but he was more than a little disappointed when Jillian left in the chaotic mass of parents picking up their kids.

Especially as she'd left without saying goodbye.

Guilt plagued Jillian the rest of the weekend. Coward, she admonished herself for the tenth time. She'd taken advantage of the confusion of departing party-goers to leave without talking to Alec again.

She'd been too afraid he'd notice how hard she was trying not to cry.

Shelby was an amazing little girl. Very bright. Perceptive. Older than her years, mostly due, Jillian suspected, to dealing with her mother's illness. Her heart had ached when Shelby had confessed her dream of becoming a doctor because she wanted to be to be just like the doctors who'd taken care of her mother.

And Shelby's hero-worship of her father was understandable as well. Clearly, Alec was as devoted to her daughter as Shelby was to him. She'd been touched at the way Shelby had included her in her generous hugs.

Tears pricked her eyes and she blinked them back with an effort. Since when had she become so emotional? When Shelby had talked about her mother's death, Jillian had remembered her own mother's pain-filled demise from MS. Granted, Jillian had been an adult when her own mother had passed away, not a young child, but listening to Shelby had made her face a harsh truth.

Until she knew what was wrong with her, she had no

business becoming close to Alec and Shelby. The last thing Shelby needed was to live through another loss.

Jillian took a deep breath and let it out slowly. Enough feeling sorry for herself. So what if she'd enjoyed the lively chaos created by the Monroe family? She should be glad to have spent a nice day with them, instead of wallowing in the uncertainty of her illness. As an only child of older parents, she'd never been exposed to the incessant teasing the Monroes had subjected each other to. She'd been secretly thrilled when they'd included her in the mix.

"So, Jillian, did my brother cry like a baby when you stitched up his wound?" Alaina had asked her. "He certainly bawled hard enough when he fell off his bike when he was ten."

"Speaking of baby, we have some interesting pictures of Alec as a baby. Mom? Do you have Alec's baby pictures handy?" Abby had added in a teasing tone. "I bet Jillian would love to see them."

Alec had taken their teasing in his stride, and even Abby had commented on it. "Alec, I can't believe how laid back you are today. Are you trying to impress Jillian or what?"

He'd simply grinned and shrugged, refusing to rise to his sister's bait. Jillian could tell they were close, although she got the impression that Alec hadn't always been as included in family gatherings as he was now.

The Monroe family had given her a couple of curious stares, but overall they'd accepted her presence at Shelby's party without question. Never before had she felt so welcomed by a large family.

At some point during the weekend she half expected Alec to call her, calling her on her rude behavior, but he didn't.

Her stomach went queasy when she realized he might very well be angry with her.

And suddenly the thought of never speaking to Alec again was unbearable. Marching to her phone, she pulled out the small scrap of paper he'd given her with his number and dialed. Relief warred with disappointment when his answering-machine kicked in.

"Alec, I'm sorry I left so quickly yesterday. Please, forgive me. Give me a call if you have time." She rattled off her number then hung up.

But even though she hung around the house, only leaving long enough to run through the park, hoping to run into him, he never returned her call.

Tuesday morning Jillian dragged herself out of bed, scrubbing the grit from her eyes as a result of her restless night.

Anxious about her evoked potential testing, she'd tossed and turned, fearing the test almost as much as the results.

She'd worked her normal shift on Monday evening, and thankfully the ED had been relatively quiet. No major trauma victims, although the steady stream of patients had kept her busy enough to make the time pass.

Annoyingly enough, she'd spent most of the night expecting Alec to drop by. She'd wondered if he thought calling was too personal and would just stop by during his shift to see how things were going.

In the bright light of morning she realized how foolish she'd been. For all she knew, Alec had worked Sunday and been off on Monday. She knew cops had to work some weekends, just like hospital staff did.

She bypassed breakfast. The instructions for the test

limited her to clear liquids which meant she couldn't even have coffee as she preferred a heavy dose of cream. On her way to the hospital, her stomach gurgled as if it were full of jumping-beans fighting against each other for a way out.

The evoked potential testing was done in the neurology clinic. She made her way to the fourth floor of the clinic building and, after checking in, took a seat in the waiting room. It felt odd to be on the other side of the clinic seating, as a patient instead of being the physician in charge.

After ten minutes, she debated going back up to the desk to remind the staff she was still waiting. Didn't they have any idea how long ten minutes was when you were sitting around, doing nothing?

"Jillian?"

She heard her name, not from the staff seated behind the clinic desk but from somewhere behind her, and swiveled in her seat. Surprised, she stared at Alec's tall, broad-shouldered frame, casually dressed in jeans and polo shirt, and the very serious expression on his face.

"Shelby?" She shot to her feet, imagining there could only be one reason for Alec to be in the hospital on his off time. "What happened to Shelby?"

He tilted his head, giving her a puzzled look. "Shelby is fine. She's spending the morning with Alaina."

Shelby was fine. Not a patient at Children's Memorial. Alec's daughter was fine. She let out her breath in a whoosh.

"Good. I'm glad." She frowned. "I don't understand. What are you doing here?"

Alec took her arm and steered her back to her seat,

meeting her gaze steadily with his. "I came here to be with you, Jillian. You mentioned this was a painful procedure and I didn't want you to face it alone."

CHAPTER EIGHT

JILLIAN stared at Alec in dazed wonder. He'd remembered the date and time of her test. Had actually come on his precious time off work just to be with her.

Ridiculous tears threatened once again, burning the backs of her eyelids. A lump formed in her throat, making speech impossible.

"I'm sorry I couldn't talk to you Sunday or Monday," Alec continued, "but I took time off work to spend a few days with Shelby." He made a face. "My sister and I took the girls to this huge doll store in Chicago and we stayed the night in a hotel. You'll be glad to know that next to her new doll, Shelby listed your doctor's bag as her favorite gift."

"I'm glad." She managed to get the words past her constricted throat. "Sounds like you had a great time."

Alec relaxed back in his seat, his expression wry. "I can't say the store had ever been on my list of places to visit, but it was worth the trip to see the excitement in Shelby's eyes. She and Bethany were in doll heaven."

Alec was a good father to Shelby. First he'd taken her to the children's tent at the festival of the arts and now this. Imagining him knee deep in myriad dolls and frilly clothes only clinched her conviction. She'd loved her father, but she'd lost him too young. She missed him. Missed the closeness Shelby shared with Alec.

"Jillian Davis?" The woman behind the desk called her name.

"Yes." She stood, disconcerted when Alec rose to his feet beside her. Clearly he'd been serious about accompanying her. "Alec, don't feel as if you need to come with me." She was somewhat embarrassed that she'd been such a chicken about this test. "I'm sure I'll be fine."

"Don't argue. I'm coming with you, and that's that." His chin was set at a stubborn angle, reminding her of Shelby.

"All right." She gave up trying to fight him, especially since she was more nervous about the test than she'd let on. Reminding herself that the shocks were only a little painful didn't help ease her anxiety. Although having Alec close by would certainly serve as a distraction.

The clinic nurse led them to a room at the end of a long hallway. Inside, there was a chair with a large machine next to it.

"Please, have a seat." The woman smiled, as if to reassure her the test would all be over in a jiffy.

Jillian reluctantly took a seat in the dentist-like chair.

"Dr. Juran will be here in a moment to explain the details of both a visual and sensory evoked potential testing. After that, I'll be back to start the procedure."

"Thanks," Jillian murmured.

When the nurse left them in the room alone, Alec reached for her hand, his long fingers engulfing hers. "Nervous?"

She lifted a shoulder. "A little," For a moment she stared at their clasped hands, unable to convince herself to let go.

"Don't worry," Alec said in a low voice. "I'll be with you the entire time."

Within moments Dr. Juran knocked on the door and came in. "Jillian, how are you?"

She tugged her fingers from Alec's so she could shake his hand. "I'm fine." When she saw his gaze landed curiously on Alec, she introduced them. "This is a friend of mine, Alec Monroe. Alec, Dr. Juran, Chief of Neurology here at Trinity Medical Center."

"Monroe, Monroe." Dr. Juran frowned at Alec. "There's a pediatrician on staff at Children's Memorial whose last name is Monroe. He recently referred an adolescent patient to me."

Alec nodded. "Adam is my brother."

"He's a good doctor." Dr. Juran sat down and turned to Jillian. "I'm planning to do both visual and sensory evoked potential testing today. The procedures have very little risk and will probably take about ninety minutes to complete."

"Why do the sensory testing?" Jillian asked. "I read how MS is diagnosed by visual testing."

"Ah, but we don't have a diagnosis of MS, do we?" Dr. Juran smiled. "Jillian, I need to do comprehensive testing if I'm to find out what is wrong with you. Please, trust me to be the neurology expert, hmm?"

She flushed, knowing he was right, and hunched her shoulders. "I will, but that doesn't mean I'm going to stop asking questions."

"I'd be disappointed if you did," he assured her. "First, Cora will attach the electrodes to your scalp. The visual testing will be first, and then we'll do the sensory testing." He must have noticed her expression because he patted her knee, as if she were a small child instead of a thirty-one-year-old woman. "The sensory testing won't take too long, I promise. I'll be as quick as possible."

She didn't doubt him. In fact, she'd researched the neurologists with the best reputation before deciding to approach Dr. Juran. "I know."

Alec didn't say much, but his presence beside her was more comforting than she'd realized. As soon as the electrodes had been attached to her scalp, he'd taken her hand firmly in his and she sensed this time he wasn't planning to let go.

The visual testing took longer than she'd thought it would. But then Cora, the nurse, informed her they were now switching to the sensory testing. Instinctively, she tightened her grip on Alec.

"Can you give her something for the pain?" he asked.

"I'm afraid not," Cora responded. "But we'll try to be quick. First we're going to start with your feet and your calves."

The first electrical shock made her suck in a harsh breath. It wasn't as bad as she'd been expecting, but not exactly comfortable either. She was more prepared for the next shock but the higher on her extremities they went, the more the shocks hurt. One painful jolt piled on top of another, increasing the sensitivity to them. When they'd finished with both of her legs, Cora moved to her arms, forcing Alec to let go.

"Talk to me," Jillian begged, gritting her teeth as she endured one electrical shock after the other. "Tell me about yourself."

Alec seemed to know exactly what she needed. "You

already know I come from a big family. I used to be known as the wild Monroe. School didn't come easy for me, so I graduated from high school with rather dismal grades. I didn't have many options so I joined the army. Considering how several members of my family were in the medical profession, I requested to be trained as a medic."

She concentrated on his words and on not yelping in pain when the electrical shock zapped a nerve she hadn't even known she had.

"Being a medic in the army is much like your job in the emergency department—you never know what injuries you'll see. After a while, though, my superiors noticed I possessed other skills that were generally more useful."

"Like what?" she asked, looking at him and concentrating on the deep, rich timbre of his voice.

"My sharpshooting skills." For a moment a dark shadow seemed to hover over his eyes. Then she thought she must have imagined it because it was gone. "They noticed how I always hit my target dead center, no matter what distance I was shooting from. So they moved me out of the medic program."

"How long were you in the army?"

"Two tours. After eight years I signed off and decided to go into law enforcement."

Too bad, because she thought he would have had a great career in the medical field.

"Why were you known as the wild Monroe?" she asked, to keep him talking and because she really wanted to know.

"I managed to get into trouble. More than anyone else in my family, that's for sure. My friend Billy and I were known for doing wacky things. One day we caught four bumblebees in a coffee-can, knocked them out with fumes from rubbing alcohol and then tied strings around them."

"Strings?" Jillian frowned. "Why?"

"Well, we took the other end of the strings and tied them around the doorhandle of the house. Soon the rubbing alcohol fumes wore off and there were four angry bees buzzing around the doorhandle. No one could go into the house or come out. Boy, was my mom mad."

She couldn't help but laugh, even as the laugh ended in a yelp.

"That was the last shock. We're finished," Cora announced.

Finally. Now that her arms were free, Alec reached over to press her hand between both of his. "Are you OK?" he murmured, his expression troubled.

She forced herself to nod. "Yeah, but I'm glad it's over."

"Me, too." He leaned forward, placing her hand on the center of his chest, directly over his heart. "Feel my heart pounding? Even though I was trying to distract you with the boring story of my life, I swear I felt every single one of those shocks as much as you did."

Looking at him, she could actually see small beads of sweat dotting his upper lip. Knowing he'd sat there, rambling about himself while empathizing with her as she'd endured the test, made her smile. "The bumblebee story was funny. Your life is hardly boring, Alec." Her smile faded. "Having you here helped more than I thought possible."

"I'm glad." He bent his head to kiss her fingers, but still didn't release her. "Remember that time you put all those stitches in me?"

She raised a brow. "Of course I do."

"You were there for me, too."

"Stitching your wound was part of my job," she pointed out. As much as she liked knowing she had been there to take care of him, it was a different situation entirely. "You being here is very different."

"Maybe," he agreed. "But I'm glad you didn't have to go through this alone."

Unable to argue that one, she simply nodded. "Thanks, Alec."

"You're welcome." He grinned, as if trying to lighten the sudden seriousness between them. "How about if we go out for lunch? I'm hungry."

How could she refuse? She fingered the residual goop in her hair from the electrodes. "After I shower."

"You look beautiful just the way you are." She wanted to laugh, but the intensity of his gaze caught her off guard. For heaven's sake, she suddenly felt beautiful, in spite of the copious amounts of white goop that had to be matted in her hair.

What was wrong with her? Being attracted to Alec wasn't part of the plan. Acting on that unmentionable attraction, like sharing another of those hot, drugging kisses, wasn't smart either. He and his daughter would be much better off if she kept their relationship light, friendly.

Yet just having him stay there with her, holding her hand and talking in that low, sexy voice of his, was not exactly the path to a light, friendly relationship. He was the type of man who stood by a woman, in both good times and bad, offering his strength and support.

For the first time in her thirty-one years she realized just what her decision to dedicate her life to her career might have cost her.

Alec picked up Jillian and took her to his favorite Mexican restaurant. "What would you like to eat? Enchiladas? Chilaquiles? Carne asada tacos, which are authentic Mexican tacos? Or my favorite chile Rellenos?"

She frowned, her freshly washed hair showing no trace of the white pasty stuff they'd used in it. "The chile Rellenos sound hot."

"They are. How about if we try a little of everything?" Taking the decision out of her hands, he ordered enough food to feed the entire ED.

The waitress hurried off with their order and he glanced at Jillian, his smile fading as he remembered how awful it had been to sit helplessly and watch while she'd suffered those electric shocks in silence. He could admit he'd been a little ticked off at the abrupt way she'd left Shelby's party, but then, when he'd gotten home from Chicago and heard her message on his answering-machine, he'd been relieved. Alaina had raised her brow when she'd heard the message and he'd inwardly groaned. Bad enough he'd had to sidestep Alaina's nosy questions about Jillian through-out the trip. Now for sure she wouldn't drop the subject.

Alaina hadn't understood why he was hesitant to bring a woman into his relationship with his daughter.

Seeing Jillian again today, he was having trouble re-membering why himself.

The food didn't take long to arrive. Jillian sniffed the

air appreciatively when the waitress arrived with her laden tray. "Smells delicious."

He had to restrain himself from leaning over to kiss her, sitting back to allow the waitress to set all the plates of food on the table.

"Have you made any progress on the percocet case?" Jillian asked, just before she took a big bite of her cheesy enchilada.

"Not much." The chile Rellenos were hot, but he liked them that way. He gulped his water, and then changed the subject, more to protect her than anything. "When are you going to hear the results of your test?"

"I'm not sure." She devoured the enchiladas and the Chilaquiles with an enthusiasm that told him she'd been just as hungry as he. "You know, Alec," she mused with a tiny frown puckering her brow, "I was thinking about what you said, about the boy who was shot being a football player. It reminded me how I treated a football player not that long ago, maybe a few weeks, because he'd severely strained his back during practice."

A spark of excitement had him reaching for his notebook. They could use a break on this case, as their secret camera hadn't turned up anything yet. The thief was obviously lying low for the moment. "What was his name?"

Jillian bit her lip as she shook her head. "I don't remember, but I'm sure I could find it in the admission logbook. I remember giving him a prescription for narcotics, though, because along with his strained neck we discovered he'd cracked a couple of ribs. Cracked ribs are extremely painful."

Her astute observations only helped to cement his

theory. Now more than ever he was certain he was on the right track.

"I remember this particular player was worried about how long I'd keep him on the injured reserve list." Jillian rubbed her temples. "He mentioned a big game scheduled for early in September." She shrugged. "I don't know the details, but it's possible the game will attract college scouts or something."

"Good point. If you do find his name, let me know." The phone at his waist vibrated and he recognized his sister's number. "Excuse me while I take this call," he murmured to Jillian. "Hi, Alaina."

"Hi, Alec. Do you think you could pick up Shelby soon? Or do you want me to take her with me to Bethany's soccer game?"

"No, I'll pick her up in a few minutes." Thankfully, it looked as if Jillian was finished eating.

"Shelby?" Jillian guessed. He was relieved she didn't seem annoyed.

"Yeah, I need to pick her up from my sister's on the way home." He snapped his phone shut. "I hope you don't mind."

"Not at all."

Alec paid for their meal and then walked with Jillian out to his car. She seemed lost in thought, and the way she worried her lower lip between her teeth made him want to cover her mouth with his to soothe her worries away. Only once he'd started nibbling on her lips, he wasn't sure he'd stop until he was completely satiated. And the way he was feeling, that could take hours. At the minimum.

Lately his body had been reminding him with an ever

constant state of arousal just how long he'd been without a woman in his life.

"So are you working second shift again tonight?" Jillian asked, after they were seated in the car.

"Yeah." He shot her a glance, as he headed for his sister's house. "You, too?"

She nodded. If he hadn't been a father with a young daughter waiting for him at home, he might have suggested they get together after their respective shifts were over. But he was a father and Shelby would be up early.

"I bet it's hard for you, working second shift while Shelby is in school," Jillian was saying. "You can't see her much during the week."

"I worked third shift most of last year, so that I could be home with her in the evenings." His body hadn't especially liked working the graveyard shift, but Shelby was more important than his sleep schedule. "If I don't get moved up to a day shift soon, I may have to go back to the night shift in September."

Then their schedules wouldn't match at all. It was obvious a relationship of any sort between them was impossible.

So why was he stuck on the idea of trying to make it work?

Jillian shifted in the passenger seat of Alec's car as he pulled into the driveway of his sister's house. She braced herself for more teasing. Would Alaina wonder what they were doing together? As it turned out, she needn't have worried because his sister was outside, waiting for them. Shelby ran over the minute they pulled up.

"Hi, Daddy. Hi, Dr. Jillian."

"Hi, yourself, munchkin." Alec didn't get out of the car, but simply waved at Alaina and waited until Shelby had climbed into the back seat before backing out of the driveway. "How was your morning?"

"Really fun. Beth and I played with our new dolls."

"Great." Alec grinned. "We're just going to drive Dr. Jillian home, all right?"

"Actually, why don't you just head home?" Jillian suggested. She felt bad, keeping Alec from the time of the day he normally spent with his daughter. He'd been kind enough to come to her test, she didn't need to intrude any longer. "I can walk from there."

"Yeah, Daddy. We can take Daisy and walk Jillian home again."

Alec nodded. "Fine with me."

Jillian had barely gotten out of the car when Shelby dashed past her toward the house to fetch her dog. In less than thirty seconds she'd come back out with Daisy on her leash. "We're ready," she announced.

Alec's phone vibrated again and he unclipped it from his waist. "I'm sorry, this is my partner. Give me a few minutes, OK?"

"Sure," she murmured.

Alec flipped open his phone and turned away, heading down the driveway obviously looking for privacy. No doubt because of some breaking news on a case. She wished he'd tell her about it, but knew he wouldn't. Jillian sat down on Alec's front porch to wait.

"Sit here beside me, Shelby," Jillian patted the empty space next to her. "Tell me, did you have fun at the doll store?"

"Yep. I got to spend the whole weekend with my daddy."
Shelby came over to sit beside her, gazing after her father.

"I bet you miss him when he's at work," Jillian
murmured, noticing Shelby's wistful gaze.

The little girl nodded. "He has to work a lot."

"I know." Jillian frowned a little. "But he still loves
you, Shelby."

"I love him, too." Shelby played with Daisy's leash.
"Jillian, is your job dangerous?"

"What?" For a moment the altercation she'd had with
Barry Cox flashed into her mind, but she shoved it away.
"No, of course not. Being a doctor is interesting, but not
dangerous."

"My daddy's job is." Shelby bent over her knees to stare
at her toes.

Uh-oh. Warning bells clamored in her head. Jillian
glanced at the girl's bent head. "Shelby, why do you say
that? Are you afraid for your daddy?"

"Sometimes," Shelby said in a muffled tone. She
glanced up at Jillian. "I overheard Aunt Abby talking about
my daddy's knife wound." Her eyes were round. "Someone
stabbed him!"

Yikes. She winced, knowing Alec wasn't going to like
hearing his daughter knew the truth. "Oh, sweetie, it's all
right." Jillian wrapped her arm around Shelby's thin shoulders and hugged her close. "Your daddy is a smart man.
He knows how to stay safe."

"I hope so." But the troubled expression in Shelby's
eyes belied her words. The girl had already lost her mother,
she knew better than anyone no one was one hundred
percent safe.

Jillian's heart broke for the little girl. "Shelby, you can talk to me any time. I'm always willing to listen. But if you're really afraid for your dad, maybe you should talk to him, too. I bet he'd like to know how you're feeling."

"Maybe." Shelby's gaze focused at a point over Jillian's shoulder and she shot off the stoop when Alec came around the corner. Just that quickly the moment was gone. "Are we ready to go?"

"You bet, munchkin." Alec held out his hand toward Shelby. His gaze met Jillian's. "Are you ready?"

"Sure." Jillian stood and fell into step beside him. This wasn't the time to tell him about the little heart-to-heart she and Shelby had shared, but he should probably know about Shelby's fears.

Soon. Tonight.

They chatted about unimportant things, but at the foot of Jillian's driveway she took his hand. "Thanks for lunch, Alec."

His surprised gaze dropped for a moment to their joined hands, then back to her face. "You're welcome."

Shelby was tugging on Daisy's leash, seeming not to be paying too much attention. "Ah, do you think we could talk more, later?" She tried to tell him with her gaze that it was important.

"Yeah. Sure." He didn't seem to get her silent message. "I'll give you a call later tonight, all right?"

"Great." She dropped his hand and turned to Shelby. "See you later, Shelby. Bye, Daisy."

"Bye, Dr. Jillian." Alec's daughter surprised her by rushing over for a quick hug. Jillian held the girl close, suddenly glad she'd been there for her.

"Later," Alec repeated, and the bright promise in his green eyes made her feel better.

Because it was very important for her to see him again. For Shelby's sake.

And, if she was honest, for hers, too. Because she was starting to care for Alec and his daughter far more than she should.

CHAPTER NINE

A FEW hours later, Jillian gazed at the whiteboard, mentally ticking off the patients listed there. Yep, she'd seen them all. Now it was time to wait for lab results, radiology results or for the next patient to come in.

Turning away from the central whiteboard, the hub of the arena, Jillian noticed Luanne was sitting alone in a corner of the nurses' station, seemingly staring out at nothing.

Concerned, Jillian crossed over. "Lu? Are you all right?"

Luanne's gaze focused on her. "I guess," her lackluster tone wasn't believable in the least.

"Hey, I know it's been really stressful around here lately." Jillian pulled up a chair so she could sit next to Luanne. "But things will get back to normal soon, you'll see."

For a moment Luanne's eyes filled with tears, but then she quickly ducked her head and swiped at her eyes. "Sorry, I don't know what's wrong with me lately."

"Do you want to talk about it?" Jillian asked.

"No." Luanne's smile was brittle. "Things won't get better until they catch whoever is stealing."

"I know." Jillian could totally relate to what Luanne

was feeling. "I hate knowing my name is on the long list of suspects, too."

"You?" Luanne shook her head. "You have a stellar reputation around here. There isn't a single person who thinks you're guilty."

Jillian wasn't so sure. And besides, it was clear when Chris had come to talk to her that he expected her to help resolve the issue. Talk about the burden of proof. "Maybe, but it still doesn't look good to have this going on while I'm the medical director."

"Tell me about it," Luanne said dryly. "Being the charge nurse isn't much easier."

Jillian didn't doubt it. This was partially what leadership was all about, taking responsibility for things you couldn't control.

Deep down, she knew Alec didn't think she was guilty, but yet at the same time he wasn't willing to discuss any details of the case with her. Not that she could really blame him, but still the knowledge rankled.

Her trauma pager went off, signaling their mini-break was over.

"Come on," she told Luanne, rising to her feet. "We have a trauma patient on the way in."

There wasn't much time to dwell on Alec, although she did hope he'd stop by some time to see her, or, at the very least, call. The heavy burden of worry his daughter carried shouldn't be shouldered alone. Somehow, without breaking Shelby's confidence, she had to convince Alec to talk to his daughter.

So much for her convictions to stay away from him. Yet even as the wry thought formed, she frowned. Did she really need to stay away? Maybe her experience with relationships was non-existent, but these feelings she harbored for Alec were worth exploring. And why couldn't she have both a family and a career? If Dr. Juran didn't find anything wrong with her, there was really no reason she couldn't make the balance between family life and work. Lots of other people did it all the time. She wouldn't be the first.

A few minutes later her patient arrived, a seventeen-year-old young man with a possible head injury resulting in seizures.

When the paramedics burst through the doors, she was totally shocked to discover Alec accompanied the patient. Was this kid part of his percocet case? The patient was certainly large enough to be a football player.

Alec must have noticed the questions in her gaze. "His name is Frank Albert and he began having seizures while we were questioning him."

She nodded, indicating she'd heard. "Luanne, make sure he has good IV access. Then draw a drug screen to make sure he doesn't have narcotics in his system," Jillian ordered.

Alec's expression was grim. "We did find percocets in his pocket. You may want to get a CT scan of his head, too. He mentioned something about having a concussion after his last football practice."

So she'd guessed right. This boy, Frank, was a football player and if Alec found percocets on him, he must be involved in this mess, too. Helpless anger on his behalf simmered in her stomach as she looked at the boy's young face. He might be a muscular kid, but he wasn't invincible, no matter what he might think. Had he taken the percocets to control the pain of his headache? At this point, until his drug screen came back, she was forced to assume so.

"I will." She stared at her patient, knowing he would be post-ictal from the seizures, making his neuro assessment useless. "Who intubated him?"

"The paramedics on the scene did," Alec informed her. "He'd stopped seizing before they arrived. I held his head, keeping his airway open until they could get the tube placed."

Alec's past experience as a medic had saved this boy's life. His skills as a medic were still right on target. Ridiculously proud of him, she nodded. "All right, let's get this kid to the CT scanner."

Luanne arranged for the scan and after a few minutes she hung up the phone and turned toward Jillian, her expression serious. "I'll take him down to Radiology."

"Good." Jillian watched as Luanne quickly wheeled the patient down the hall, where the radiology department was located not far from the ED.

"Did you learn anything from Frank before he started to seize?" Jillian asked Alec in a low tone when they were finally alone. "Like who gave him the pills?"

Slowly Alec shook his head. "Not as much as I would have liked. He admitted to taking the percocets, heck, he threw them at me, claiming they didn't work anyway. Moments after that he fell to the ground in a full grand mal seizure. I suspect even percocets couldn't help the pain in his head if his head injury was getting worse."

"No, probably not." The idea of someone taking advantage of these kids by providing illegal drugs made her feel sick. "Sounds like he should have come in for treatment right away."

A dark shadow fell over Alec's eyes. "Yeah, no kidding."

She fell silent for a moment, wondering just what Frank's scan would show. "Frank was lucky you showed up to question him."

"It was our second time through. I'm convinced the kids know something but they sure aren't talking."

That wasn't good news at all. "I hope you get one of them to crack soon."

"We will. No matter what it takes." He sounded confident, looked almost invincible with his blue uniform, his shield and the gun on his hip.

He was very capable, yet she knew only too well he was only flesh and blood beneath the uniform. Hadn't she already stitched him up once?

Didn't he realize just how worried Shelby was about his safety?

Glancing around to make sure she wasn't needed, Jillian lowered her voice and suggested, "Alec, I know it's none of my business, but maybe once this case is over, you should consider finding a less dangerous job."

Alec stared, shocked by her abrupt change of subject. "What? Why?"

Her gaze skittered from his. "Think about the danger you're constantly exposed to. There must be other positions within the Milwaukee Police Department that would be less risky."

Annoyed, he hated to admit she was right. At one time he'd considered taking the detective's exam. But that had been a long time ago. But his life wasn't her business. What on earth had possessed Jillian to bring this up now? "I'm not really in that much danger. Smart cops enjoy long, healthy careers."

Jillian crossed her arms protectively over her chest, her gaze still troubled. "Shelby needs you, Alec. She's already lost one parent, she doesn't need to lose another."

Anger spiked, hot and swift. "I love my daughter. I'd never do anything to hurt her."

"Not on purpose," Jillian agreed. "But don't you realize how much she depends on you?"

Yes, he did. He loved Shelby with his whole heart, but sometimes the thought of how dependent she was on him for her wellbeing was scary. No matter what he did for a living, the responsibility of being a parent wouldn't go away.

Still, his career wasn't always dangerous and he refused to feel guilty for having a job he loved. "Firefighters are injured in the line of duty more often than cops are." Then a horrible thought occurred to him. "Did Shelby tell you she was worried about me being hurt on the job?"

Jillian hesitated, and then nodded in relief. "Yes. I'm sorry, I had to tell you. I don't want to break her confidence, but you need to talk to her, Alec. Somehow she overheard your family talking about your knife wound. She knows you were stabbed."

Damn. His gut clenched. He hadn't wanted that fact to slip out. Troubled by the news, he slowly nodded. "I'll talk to her. I don't want her to be scared."

"Hey, she's probably thinking the worst because she lost her mother." Jillian might be trying to make him feel better but it wasn't working.

Because that was exactly the point.

"Dr. Davis? Your seizure patient is on his way back from the CT scan."

"Thanks." Jillian lightly squeezed Alec's arm. "I'm sorry. I'm sure Shelby will be fine after you two talk."

"I hope so," he muttered, watching her walk away.

As Jillian headed over to meet her patient, he scanned the people working in the trauma bay, trying to put names to faces from the list they'd compiled. He and Rafe had interviewed all the employees on the list and had four names that topped their list of suspects. Three nurses had close ties to members of the Barclay Park football team.

Jillian would hate knowing a few of her coworkers were suspects. Especially because she worked with them every day.

When Luanne wheeled Frank Albert back into the trauma bay, he noticed Jillian immediately stepped up to take over the patient's care, demanding a neurosurgery consult for the boy.

"What's going on?" he asked, walking over.

"He has a major hemorrhage into his brain." Jillian's face was tense as she ordered medications he'd never heard of, like Lasix and mannitol. "If they don't operate, he'll die."

Stepping back, he gave Jillian and her staff plenty of room to work. He knew that if anyone could save this kid's life, it was Jillian Davis. He'd been impressed with her the first time he'd met her, but over these past few weeks he'd only grown more in awe of her talent and ability. Finally she'd gotten hold of the neurosurgeon, who took one look at the CT scan Jillian held up before his eyes and then ordered the patient to be taken straight to surgery.

Only once Frank Albert was safe in the neurosurgeon's hands did Jillian seem to remember he was there. She came back toward him. "They're going to operate. But his chances aren't great," she cautioned.

"I know." He didn't like the thought that this boy might be one of those kids he couldn't save. They haunted him, the ones he lost. Such a waste of a young life. Shaking his head, he glanced at his watch, surprised it was barely eight p.m. "I need to get going. Rafe and I still have a long shift ahead of us."

"Are you all right?" Her questioning gaze sought his.

"Yeah." Once he'd gotten over the shock of what Jillian had told him, he realized he was glad to know how Shelby really felt. He curled his fingers into his palms to keep from reaching for her. "Jillian? Do you mind if I stop by later?"

She stared at him for a moment and he wished he knew what she was thinking behind those sparkling blue eyes of hers. Finally she gave him a small smile. "I'd like that."

"Good." He watched her as she crossed the room to where a patient was waiting to be seen. He loved how she looked so serious when taking care of her patients.

Earlier that day, he'd found Shelby playing doctor with her dolls, including her new one. Trust his daughter to take an expensive doll and wrap gauze around her head, making the doll into a patient. He knew lots of kids played doctor or nurse, but he couldn't help hoping this was a sign his daughter really would pursue a career in medicine. Jillian was a great role model for his daughter.

No way did he want Shelby to follow in his footsteps and be a cop. Just thinking about his daughter learning to shoot a gun was enough to make his skin crawl.

Maybe Jillian was right. Maybe he did need to look into a more stable, less dangerous career.

As he went outside to meet Rafe, he wondered just what it meant that his daughter had chosen Jillian, rather than one of his sisters, to confide in.

* * *

Jillian saw several new patients and followed up on previous ones, but throughout the next few hours her trauma patient, Frank Albert, dominated her thoughts.

At one point, when she couldn't stand not knowing for a second longer, she picked up the phone and dialed the number for the operating suite.

"Frank Albert is still in surgery," the nurse informed her.

Jillian ground her teeth together in frustration, but kept her voice pleasant. "Yes, I figured that much. How is he doing?"

"The neurosurgeon has requested a neuro ICU bed for him."

Yeah, that much she'd also figured out all by herself. Striving for patience, she went for specifics. "How are his vital signs? Is his blood pressure elevated? How fast is his pulse?"

"His pulse and his blood pressure are both high." The nurse obviously didn't want to go into details. "Why don't you follow up once he's transferred to the ICU? They're talking about sending him up within the next thirty minutes."

"Thanks. I'll do that." She hung up and closed her eyes for a moment in despair. High blood pressure and pulse were both a sign of impending brain herniation. There was a very good chance Frank could die. If only he'd sought medical treatment sooner, maybe his life wouldn't be hanging by a frayed thread.

Pulling herself together, she spun away from the phone and threw herself into work. There were plenty of other patients in her ED who weren't hovering on the brink of death. Better for her to concentrate on those she could help fix rather than those she couldn't.

At least Alec hadn't been too upset about Shelby. He

was the type of guy who would always put his daughter's needs first.

Not that she minded. His loving attitude toward his daughter was one of the things she admired most about him. Listening to Shelby describe her fears about Alec being hurt had nearly made her cry.

A few hours later, near the end of her shift, Jillian took the elevators up to the fifth floor where the neuro intensive care unit was located.

She didn't go into Frank Albert's room, though, because his bed was surrounded by sobbing family members.

Feeling sick, she found the nurse. "What happened?"

"He's not doing well." The nurse's eyes were red and puffy as if she'd shed a few tears with the family. "We're going to try this new hypothermia treatment but we've also prepared the family for the possibility of brain death."

Not good news, but nothing she hadn't suspected. There was always a chance he'd pull through, especially with this new hypothermia protocol, but it was a slim chance. Jillian's vision blurred and she quickly blinked back tears. "Thanks for letting me know."

Turning on her heel, she went back downstairs, hoping very much that Alec had arrived.

Alec finished his shift. He debated going home to change his clothes, but didn't want to miss the chance of seeing Jillian. He also wanted to know how Frank Albert was faring.

Besides, if he went home, he'd have to explain to Meagan, the college girl he'd hired to watch Shelby, why he was changing his clothes and going back out. As if he didn't already feel guilty enough, sneaking over to see

Jillian for a few minutes. Even though he knew full well Shelby was sleeping and that she wouldn't miss him in the least, the guilt was still there, niggling.

Throwing the car into Park, he rested his forehead on the steering wheel. Was he crazy to be here? What if Jillian had to work late? How long would he stick around, waiting?

As long as it took to see her, he acknowledged grimly.

Man, he was in serious trouble. Pulling himself together, he slid out from behind the wheel of his car. As he walked toward the entrance of the emergency department, he saw Jillian walking out.

She'd taken off her lab coat and had taken her hair down from the tie holding it away from her face. The moment he saw her, his heart skipped in his chest. Her gaze met his and he saw relief and the shadow of grief, her lips trembling slightly as she tried to smile.

He quickened his pace as she continued walking toward him. She never hesitated when he hauled her close in a welcoming hug.

Neither one of them spoke yet they moved in silent harmony. He lowered his mouth to hers, claiming her with a deep kiss.

She wrapped her arms around his neck and kissed him back as if she needed this moment with him more than anything on earth. He groaned when she clutched him tight, his tongue mating with hers. It was as if they had both been starving, craving this physical contact since they'd parted earlier that day.

Somehow, he wasn't sure how, he managed to maneuver them to his car. Lifting her up so she was sitting on the hood, he pressed his body against hers, cupping her face in his hands. When he could force himself to stop kissing her, he leaned his forehead against hers.

"Jillian." His voice held a ragged edge he couldn't hide. "Stop me if this isn't what you want."

"Alec, wait." She gulped, taking a deep breath and pulling away to look into his eyes. "I need to tell you something. Frank Albert isn't doing so well. There's a good chance he'll..." She couldn't finish.

"I know." He'd suspected Frank might not make it. "I'm sorry."

"Me, too." She buried her face against his neck. "Hold me."

"I will." He cuddled her close, wishing the night didn't have to end. But he couldn't very well invite her over to his place for the night, because his daughter was sleeping there.

And he couldn't very well go to her place, because Meagan needed to get home as she had a summer class in the early afternoon.

"For now," he amended softly. He felt her stiffen in his arms and knew she was upset by his response.

Damn. He never should have come back here tonight, starting something he couldn't finish.

CHAPTER TEN

FOR now? Sharp disappointment stabbed deep. Until the moment Alec had caught her up in his arms, kissing her like there was no tomorrow, she hadn't realized just how much she needed this.

Needed him.

Because at this moment she didn't really care about all the logical reasons she shouldn't be there with him. In the darkness it was too easy to imagine they were the only two people on the face of the earth.

Heavens, when was the last time her body ached with need like this? She couldn't remember feeling this edgy longing to be joined as one with someone, with Alec. None of the men she'd dated in the past had made her feel this way. Special. Desirable. Passionate.

She didn't want him to leave. Not just yet. Not when all her emotions were so raw.

"I— Damn it, Jillian. I want to be with you more than anything, but I can't tonight." The harsh lines of pure agony grooving his face soothed her disappointment a little. "I'm sorry, I didn't mean for this to get so out of control."

Since she understood he wasn't the kind of man to take

a relationship lightly, especially considering the added complication of his daughter, she swallowed her regret and nodded. "I know. It's all right."

He let out a harsh laugh. "Hell, no, it's not all right." He cradled her cheek in his hand, stroking his thumb against the curve of her jaw. "It really, really isn't all right. Do you have any idea how much I want you?"

If it was anything like how she felt at the moment, she did. Although was she really ready to take this step? Maybe it was for the best. She tried to smile, then turned her head to kiss his hand. "I understand. You have to get home, for Shelby."

He closed his eyes and let out a jagged sigh. "Yes." Then his eyes flew open. "Wait a minute, Thursday! What are you doing on Thursday night?"

"Thursday?" she repeated, trying to think past the haze of desire. "What's Thursday?"

"I just remembered, Shelby has a Brownie Girl Scout camp on Thursday. My sister Alaina is taking the girls and they're staying overnight." His entire face lit up with un-suppressed hope. "She'll be gone most of Friday."

Jillian slid off the hood of Alec's car, catching her breath at the implication. Not only could they spend the night together Thursday, but they had all day Friday prior to work as well to be together. A tiny part of her regretted the need to make plans around his daughter's schedule but, then again, could she really blame him? She wouldn't care about Alec if he was the sort of guy who could easily drop his daughter off someplace just so he could spend time with a woman.

Even if she happened to be the woman in question.

And besides, hadn't she experienced more than one

fantasy about waking up in Alec's arms, sharing breakfast in bed? Maybe a portion of her fantasy would come to fruition.

"I don't have plans for Thursday," she acknowledged in a soft voice.

"You do now." Alec caught her close in an exuberant hug. He let her go quickly and took a step back, holding up his hands as if forcing himself to keep his distance. "If I touch you again, I won't be able to walk away," he murmured. "I'll see you, Thursday, OK? Promise me? I'll see you Thursday?"

She laughed at the comical mixture of hope and longing in his eyes and nodded. "It's a date."

Alec was tormented by thoughts of kissing Jillian that night as he tried to sleep. He tossed and turned for hours, before finally falling into a restless slumber. What seemed like moments later, Shelby jumped into his bed with Daisy, to wake him up.

"Daddy, don't be such a sleepyhead!" No soft, gentle patting of his cheek this morning, Shelby bounced on the mattress, full of energy, as if intending to jar him awake. "Wake up, Daddy! You promised to make French toast and bacon this morning for breakfast!"

Had he? He groaned. Must have sounded like a good idea at the time. Prying one eye open, he tried to read the luminous dials on his alarm clock. Seven a.m. Guess it could have been worse. Suppressing a pathetic moan, he pulled himself upright. "I'm awake." Or he would be once he downed a pot of coffee.

He stumbled to the kitchen, heading straight for the coffee-maker as Shelby began to help him assemble the ingredients for their breakfast. Despite his fatigue, he couldn't help but grin, knowing in less than two days he'd see Jillian again. Thirty-six hours and counting. Every nerve in his body hummed with the anticipation of spending some quality time alone with her. *Get a grip*, he warned himself as his body tightened at the thought.

"What's so funny, Daddy?" Shelby asked, her head tipped to one side.

Realizing he probably looked like an idiot, grinning at his secretly lecherous thoughts, he tried to rein himself in as he glanced at his daughter. "Nothing is funny, munchkin. I'm just happy."

"I like it when you're happy," Shelby announced.

Her innocent remark stopped him cold.

Shelby liked it when he was happy. Being with Jillian made him happy. Yesterday Shelby had played doctor and had asked when they were going to see Jillian again. He'd mentioned going to the park over the weekend, promising to stop by to see if Jillian was home.

So why had he been so worried about seeing Jillian on a regular basis? There was no reason to think Shelby would be traumatized by him having a relationship with Jillian. Jillian fit perfectly into his life. If anything, his daughter would only benefit from the added security of a happy family.

Emphasis on family.

Shelby already used Jillian as a confidante. He still needed to sit her down to talk about her fears. But, that aside, he noticed Shelby dropping hints on how much she wished she had a sister or brother to play with, like her cousin Bethany, who had a younger brother, Ben. Shelby would be delighted if he were to have a child with Jillian.

A baby. With Jillian.

A fist squeezed in his chest, making it hard to breathe. He set down his double-strength coffee without tasting a drop. Wide awake now, without the benefit of chemical stimulation, he sank into a kitchen chair.

Somehow, without meaning to, he'd fallen in love with Dr. Jillian Davis.

Jillian overslept on Thursday morning. Unusual for her, as she happened to be a naturally early riser, but she easily rationalized that it must be her body's way of compensating for the sleep she probably wouldn't get later that night.

The mere thought of spending the entire night with Alec made her blush. Good grief, should she pack an overnight bag? Her toothbrush and comb? A hairdryer? Would he look at her oddly, wondering if she planned to move in?

Probably. OK, no overnight bag. She wasn't moving in with the man. This was just a date. A very intimate date. Had he even mentioned food? Most dates at least made a pretense out of having dinner or going to a movie.

She couldn't have cared less about a movie. She didn't want to waste time alone with Alec watching some tedious film. Dinner might have been nice, although by the time they both got off work, it would be too late to eat.

Why was she obsessing about the details?

Maybe because she'd never in her whole life made a date for the sole purpose of having sex.

Irritated with herself for over-analyzing things, she shoved the gnawing worry aside and jumped into the shower. As she was finishing her brunch—no sense in eating breakfast when it was close to noon—her phone rang.

Wondering if the caller was Alec, she jumped for it, nearly knocking over her glass of milk in the process.

"Hello, may I speak to Jillian Davis?"

Jillian frowned when she didn't recognize the voice. "This is she."

"Jillian, my name is Barbara Evans and I'm Dr. Juran's new administrative assistant. I'm calling to let you know the results of your evoked potential testing were negative."

"Negative?" Dazed, Jillian sank back into her kitchen chair. So much had happened, she'd forgotten all about the test results. She could hardly believe the news. Her results were actually negative?

"Give Dr. Juran a call if you have any questions, OK?" Barbara added.

"I will." Jillian set the cordless handset on the table. Then she leaped up and did a little cha-cha step. Her results were negative. This had to mean for sure she didn't have multiple sclerosis!

Laughter bubbled up in her throat and she reached again for her phone, desperately needing to share the news with someone. Instinctively, she dialed Alec's number.

He wasn't home, but when his answering-machine clicked on, she left him a message. "Alec, it's Jillian. We have something to celebrate tonight! I just found out the results of my evoked potential tests are negative! Can't wait to see you later. Bye."

Feeling slightly foolish, she hung up. Maybe Alec wouldn't really understand the implications of her negative results, but that was OK. Having someone you cared enough for to share the good news with was all that mattered.

Jillian headed to the ED to work her shift full of breath-less anticipation for the evening to come.

As soon as she arrived at work, Jillian realized her good mood was a bit premature. The atmosphere in the ED was tense. Not a single staff member was smiling. The easy camaraderie and light banter had vanished. Susan, the nurse who'd taken care of her burn patient, looked particularly bad, her face pale and her sunken eyes surrounded by dark circles.

As they were busy with patients, she didn't get a chance to talk to Susan until things quieted down, toward the end of their shift.

Finally she got her chance, when she found Susan standing alone at one end of the nurses' station in the arena.

"Susan?" Jillian hoped the woman wasn't coming down with flu. "Are you feeling all right?"

Susan lifted a shoulder, but didn't meet her gaze, pre-tending to be engrossed in the chart in front of her. "Fine."

Susan didn't look fine. She looked stressed. Or upset, as if she hadn't slept in a week. "Is something bothering you? Do you need to talk?"

"No." Susan was uncharacteristically abrupt, her closed expression didn't invite further discussion. She closed the chart and stalked off, her back stiff.

Surprised, Jillian watched her go.

"I heard the cops have been questioning her because her son plays for the Barclay Park football team." The smirk on Wayne Netter's face made her want to slap him.

Susan? The source of the narcotic thefts? No, she didn't believe it.

As much as she would have liked to ignore Wayne, she

needed to give him a report. From the corner of her eye she caught sight of Alec, standing off in the corner of the ED. A glance at the clock confirmed he was early. He didn't look at all impatient, quite the contrary. He leaned against the wall as if he had all the time in the world.

Did he think she was going to leave without him?

The thought almost made her laugh. Hardly. She sent Alec a give-me-a-minute smile and turned to Wayne. "Would you like a rundown of the patients who need to be seen?"

"I'm sure I can figure it out on my own," he sneered. "I don't need your help."

Well. Talk about tense. Jillian pursed her lips at Wayne's nasty tone. Deciding his comment wasn't worthy of a response, she turned to the patient whiteboard. "There are two patients still waiting for diagnostic testing to determine their disposition, Jennifer Walden in room twenty-one and Mark Robbins in room eight."

She was determined to give him a concise report, so he wouldn't be able to claim down the road something was her fault because she hadn't given him some bit of information. She didn't trust Wayne as far as she could spit. "You'll need to check their radiology reports before they can be cleared. There are three patients currently on the admission list waiting for bed assignments, and there are another four patients we're waiting for lab results on." She swung back to meet his bored gaze. "Any questions?"

"No." He turned on his heel and walked away.

For a moment she marveled at his rudeness, then shook off her irritation. Wayne's crankiness couldn't ruin her evening.

She was free to go.

In her office, she picked up her purse and quickly locked her office door behind her. Alec was still waiting just outside the ED doors.

"Hi," she greeted him, feeling awkward.

"Hi, yourself." He grinned and she immediately relaxed when he pulled a bouquet of daisies out from behind his back. "I don't know what your favorite flower is, but these happened to be growing in my garden. I hope you don't mind."

She could easily imagine him picking his own flowers to give to her. Burying her nose in the blooms, she said, "Thank you, Alec. They're beautiful."

He pulled her into his arms for a quick kiss. "You're a woman who deserves roses or orchids, but I didn't have any of those available."

She was surprised by his comment because she didn't particularly care for roses or orchids, but then he was taking her hand and tugging her toward the parking lot. "Let's go. Do you want to follow me in your car?"

"Yes, I'll follow you." She decided not to remind him she'd been at his house more than once and therefore knew exactly where it was. The hint of nervousness surrounding him made her feel better.

The trip to his house from the medical center took less than ten minutes. She pulled into his driveway, wondering if he had nosy neighbors who would notice her car being there all night. Should she move it? What if one of them said something to Shelby?

Alec came over to open her door as she gathered her purse and her bouquet of daisies, glancing into her back seat. "Ah, anything else?"

Like an overnight bag? Now she wished she had packed the darn thing. "No. I, uh, didn't have time."

"That's all right, I have plenty of extra stuff if you need anything." Alec didn't seem to mind as he escorted her inside.

She sucked in a surprised breath when she saw his kitchen table was laid out with place settings for two.

"Make yourself comfortable," he told her as he lit two tapered candles standing in the center of the table. "Are you hungry? I usually have something light to eat when I get home."

She was touched by the effort he'd obviously put into preparing for their evening together. "Maybe a little," she admitted.

"It's nothing fancy, just some grilled salmon, but I thought we should have something solid to go with this." He pulled a bottle of icy-cold champagne, along with two chilled glasses, out of his fridge. He quickly popped the cork on the champagne and poured them each a glass. "Here's to your good news—negative test results. And to us."

To us? She could only murmur something unintelligible as she touched her glass to his and then took a sip. The champagne was delicious as it glided down her throat and if she wasn't careful, the alcohol could go straight to her head.

She didn't want her mind fuzzy from alcohol. She wanted to remember every detail in sharp clarity. To savor these moments with Alec.

Setting her glass down, she took a step toward him and smoothed her fingers over the starched fabric of his navy-blue uniform shirt. "Will dinner be ruined if we don't eat until much later?"

CHAPTER ELEVEN

ALEC was sure he should say something smart. Intelligent. Maybe he wasn't the college graduate she was but he was darned if he'd ever considered himself stupid.

But that's how he felt at the moment. Idiotic. Dumb. Unable to formulate a single coherent sentence. Her hands on his chest, even with the barrier of his shirt between them, were driving him crazy. He struggled to respond.

"I— No. Yes. I mean, later is good. Fine." When she flashed that sexy smile his tongue knotted, so he gave up, deciding to let actions speak for him. Pulling her close, he dipped his head to taste her.

Heavens, she tasted amazing. Like chocolate, raspberries and ice cream, all his favorite desserts rolled into one. And when she melted against him, he knew if they didn't move soon, *now*, they'd end up right there, on the kitchen floor. Not that he minded the floor, but Jillian deserved better.

A bed. Soft mattress. Her rounded softness beneath him.

Take it easy, Monroe, he warned himself, there was no rush, you have all night.

Yet suddenly all night didn't seem long enough.

"Jillian," he murmured, trying to draw away long

enough to get his bearings. Which way was his bedroom? "Are you sure? Absolutely sure about this?" There, the hallway leading to his bedroom was straight ahead.

"Yes, Alec." She pressed her mouth against his neck, right over his carotid pulse, and he figured she knew how hard his heart was pounding. When she bit him lightly, he shivered and groaned. "I'm sure."

Enough. He couldn't take another second. Lifting her in his arms, he strode down the hall toward his bedroom. Without bothering to kick the door shut behind him, he carried her to the side of his bed then gently lowered her to her feet.

He itched to rip her clothes off, but cradled her face in his hands, trying to bank the fire raging within. "Jillian, I've wanted you from the moment we first met, all those months ago when I was lucky enough to have the sexiest doctor in the ED stitching up my wound."

"I remember," she murmured, her fingers busily undoing the buttons of his shirt. "I never forgot you either, the hot police officer injured in the line of duty."

Hot? She'd considered him hot? Heck, if he'd known that, maybe he would have gone out of his way to see her sooner. Jillian finished with his buttons and tugged his shirt from the waistband of his pants.

He gladly helped her divest himself of his shirt but then turned his attention to her scrubs. The thin cotton was hardly much of a barrier, but soon she wore only a tiny raspberry red bra and panties, looking so good he was sure he'd died and gone to heaven.

When his hands went to his belt buckle, she stared and he wanted to ignore the twinge of uncertainty he saw in her eyes. He unhooked his belt and let his pants drop, his gun and cuffs making a metallic thud as they hit the floor. He kicked them off—when had he lost his shoes?—then faced her wearing a pair of navy blue boxers that didn't come close to hiding his arousal.

"Changed your mind?" he forced himself to ask, reaching out to rub his thumb across her bottom lip.

She brought her gaze to his and smiled. "No. I haven't changed my mind. But you should know, it's been a long time for me."

For a moment he couldn't breathe, his body, impossibly, hardened further. He wanted her so badly he couldn't move. As he watched, she reached up and unhooked the front clasp of her bra, opening the edges and exposing her beautiful breasts.

He knew in that moment he didn't deserve anyone this perfect, but he also knew that no matter what he wasn't giving her up. For some reason she was here, which meant she belonged to him and he was going to keep her and cherish her forever.

"Jillian," he murmured. He stripped off the boxers. His over-inflated ego didn't need the added stimulus of her quickly indrawn breath, and he picked her up and placed her in the center of his bed. Stretching out beside her, he bent to kiss her breast, but his intent to go slow vaporized the moment she caught his hard length in her hand.

He had condoms close at hand, thank heavens. Within seconds he was poised, ready to take her, and he stared down at her, the words *I love you* lodged in his throat.

"Please, Alec," she begged, oblivious to his turmoil. Wrapping her legs around his hips, she urged him on. "I want you. Now, please!"

He moaned low in his throat and thrust deep, pure pleasure stealing his breath. He kissed her, knowing he wouldn't last long the way she moved beneath him, rotating her hips, seeking her own pleasure. He felt beads of sweat form at his temples as he drew out the moment, using everything he had, his mouth and his hands to bring her to climax before he lost the last vestiges of his control.

When she cried out his name, her body shuddering with the spasms of her release, he quickened his pace, joining her moments later. Gathering her close, he rolled to his side to spare her the pressure of his weight.

For a long moment he couldn't move, couldn't think, satiated with Jillian's scent filling his head. Then he opened one eye to peer at the clock, trying to see the time.

Just after twelve-thirty a.m. His mouth quirked in a grin. Good. They still had the rest of the night.

And if he had his way, the night would last longer than a few hours. It would last for ever.

Jillian snuggled against Alec, listening to the steady beat of his heart beneath her ear, stunned by the urge to laugh and to cry at the same time.

She loved him.

To be fair, she'd known her feelings were more than casual for a long time now, but tonight, after the effort he'd put into their date and his tender yet passionate love-making, she faced the truth full force.

She loved him.

Closing her eyes, she fought the warring emotions flipping in her chest. On one hand, she finally felt free, in control of her future, grabbing these moments with Alec in both hands. Yet her emotional response to his love-making, realizing she'd fallen in love, only proved she wasn't in control at all. Silly maybe, but no man had ever touched her the way Alec had.

Imagining a future with Alec was a very real pos-sibility, now that she knew her evoked potential tests were negative.

A future with Alec and Shelby.

Satisfied, she slowly relaxed. Loving Alec wouldn't seem so overwhelming if she took things one day at a time.

Her brief euphoria was shattered when the doorbell rang. Twice. Alec lifted his head with a dark frown. "What the heck?"

"Shelby?" she asked.

His eyes widened and he lunged for his clothes, yanking his jeans on with abrupt movements. "Must be Alaina," he murmured. "No one else would stop over at this time of night."

She discreetly held the sheet to her chin as she reached for her discarded clothes, not that she needed to bother, Alec wasn't so much as glancing in her direction. Before she could say anything else, he pulled a T-shirt over his head and headed down the hall to answer the door.

She took the time to get dressed too, before following him out to the living room.

"What happened?" Alec asked, as he took Shelby from Alaina's arms.

"She threw up her dinner, she probably has flu." Alaina's keen gaze didn't miss Jillian standing there. "I did call but there was no answer. How are you, Jillian?"

"Fine." She glanced between Alec and Alaina. Did Alec

mind that his sister had seen her? Alaina wasn't stupid, she had to know what she'd interrupted. Hopefully, Shelby was young enough not to think twice about Jillian being there with her dad.

Maybe.

"Daddy, I'm sick," Shelby mumbled, lifting her head from his shoulder. "I don't like throwing up."

"I know, munchkin, no one likes to be sick." Alec cradled her close. "It's OK, you're home now."

"See you later, Alec. Jillian." Alaina covered her mouth as she yawned. "I brought Bethany back too and I need to get her home. Hope she doesn't come down with it next."

"I hope not, too." Alec grimaced. Alaina lifted her hand in a wave as she headed outside.

"Daddy, my tummy hurts again." Shelby's tone changed to a whimper.

"Do you have a bucket?" Jillian feared Shelby might throw up. "And some towels?"

"Somewhere in the basement, I think." He looked indecisive for a moment, then said, "Will you take her for a minute? I'll go look for the bucket and towels."

"Sure." Luckily, Shelby didn't seem to mind when Alec transferred her over to Jillian's arms. The little girl was warm, probably running a low-grade fever. Shelby's arms snaked around her neck, clinging to her. Jillian headed to the sofa, smoothing a hand down Shelby's back. "It's OK, Shelby. Your daddy will be back soon."

"Ooh, my tummy hurts." Jillian could tell she was having stomach cramps the way Shelby twisted against her. If Alec didn't get back soon, the poor child was liable to throw up all over his sofa.

"I know, sweetie." Jillian continued to soothe Shelby as the girl moved restlessly against her.

"Found one. Thanks." Alec returned to the living room, his arms laden with a bucket and towels. "I'll be right back." He went down the hall to his room, returning after a few seconds. When he held out his arms for Shelby, Jillian transferred the little girl over with regret.

She stood there, feeling awkward as Alec took Shelby down the hall to his bedroom. She didn't mind staying to help, but Alec seemed as if he had everything under control.

He emerged from the bedroom a few minutes later. "I'm sorry things turned out this way, Jillian."

"It's all right. Poor Shelby. She looks miserable."

"Yeah." He sighed and rubbed a hand over his neck. "I'm going to lie down next to her, see if she can get some sleep."

"All right." She figured he was politely telling her it was time to leave. She picked up her purse off the end table. "Goodnight, Alec."

He walked her to the door, and then pulled her close for a quick kiss. "I'll call you," he said softly.

"OK." She tried to smile as she opened the door and stepped outside. She climbed into her car and drove home, trying not to be too disappointed.

She would have stayed, helping Shelby through this. But maybe Alec wasn't thinking of a future the way she was.

He'd promised to call. Maybe she was making a big deal out of nothing. She'd see him again soon. Shelby would get over her flu bug in a few days.

Although it was doubtful that Shelby would have another overnight camp to attend any time soon. Making love to Alec had been special, but Jillian couldn't help feeling a little sad he hadn't asked her to stay to help take care of Shelby.

Alec sat beside his daughter, staring down at her sleeping face. After she'd gotten sick one more time, she'd finally fallen into a restless sleep.

How could he have forgotten about the responsibilities of being a father, even for a second? When the doorbell had rung, twice, he'd almost dismissed it as a kid's prank. He'd assumed Shelby would be fine with his sister.

No, actually, it was more than just an assumption. Deep down, he hadn't wanted his night with Jillian to end. Not like this. Not so abruptly.

Heck, it wasn't as if he'd been actually sleeping. Just making love to Jillian.

Should he have asked her to stay? He wasn't sure if she had really wanted to help or had just been her normally kind self. Truthfully, he'd felt lousy enough, calling such an abrupt halt to their night together, that he hadn't wanted to take advantage of Jillian by making her sit with his sick daughter all night.

Or had he been trying to protect Shelby from knowing he'd spent the night with Jillian?

Maybe a little of both, he grudgingly admitted. Shelby was too young to understand the implication of Jillian spending the night but, regardless, he didn't plan on being the type of father who'd allow his girlfriends to spend the night in front of his daughter.

Besides, Jillian had to work the next day, as did he, so it wasn't fair to expect her to spend the night with a sick kid. He might have to call off work himself to take care of Shelby. Unless she was feeling better and Meagan wouldn't mind staying with her. Either way, though, it wasn't as if Jillian had signed up for being a surrogate parent.

As he listened to his daughter's even breathing, Alec stared at the ceiling and thought about how nice it would have been to have Jillian there with him for emotional support.

As if they were a family.

The next day, Jillian heard from Alec just as she was about to leave the house for work.

"Hi, Alec." She was very glad he'd called as he'd promised. "How's Shelby?"

"Better. She hasn't thrown up in almost five hours." Alec sounded tired—she'd bet he hadn't gotten much sleep. "If she keeps down the chicken soup I've given her, I might still go to work."

"Kids tend to get over illness much faster than adults do," she agreed. "I'm sure she'll be fine."

"I'm really sorry, Jillian," Alec said in a low tone. "I felt awful ending our night together like that."

His apology was so sincere she immediately hastened to reassure him. "Alec, it's not as if you planned for Shelby to get sick. I understand, really. It's all right."

He sighed. "Yeah, well, I don't think it's all right, but there's nothing I can do now. The other reason I called is because Rafe has gotten a break in the case. I just wanted you to know ahead of time that things might be crazy for a while."

He sounded as if he was worried he might be busy. She was touched he cared enough to let her know. "I under-stand." Jillian really wanted to know more but swallowed the questions bubbling in her throat. Poor Susan, the nurse whose son was on the Barclay Park football team, didn't look as if she could take much more. As tense as things were in the ED, Jillian hoped Alec and Rafe found the guilty person soon.

Alec hesitated a moment, and then continued, "Jillian, I'd like to see you again. We're having a family barbeque at my parents' house this weekend—would you be willing to come with us? Me and Shelby?"

She caught her breath, knowing that if she agreed to go there would be no hiding their relationship. This was Alec's way of including her in the warm embrace of his family. The Monroes had given her the once-over already, a second date would seal her status as Alec's girlfriend without question. Was she ready for this step?

Yes. Absolutely. "I'd love to."

"Great." Alec's relief was evident in his tone. "I'll call you later with the details."

"Sounds good." Jillian hung up, realizing she'd just taken a gigantic step toward admitting to the world how she felt about him. Doubts instantly assailed her and she pushed them away with determination.

There was really no reason she couldn't have it all. A career and a family. A beautiful stepdaughter.

And, most importantly, Alec's love.

The ED was quiet until about nine o'clock that night, then the gates opened and a flood of patients poured in.

First Jillian dealt with two victims of a motor-vehicle crash. Luckily, they had both been wearing their seatbelts so their injuries could have been much worse. A few broken limbs were nothing compared to massive head and internal injuries.

The numbness and tingling sensations had returned to her right hand. When the traction bar had slipped from her fingers, thankfully bouncing off the mattress of the bed, she'd been forced to step back and let the nurses finish setting up the traction.

Once she'd gotten the two patients admitted onto the orthopedic trauma service, she received another call about a drug overdose patient. Ignoring her concern over the symptoms in her hand, she headed back to the trauma bay. The cleaning fluid on the floor was barely dry when the double doors slammed open again.

The patient was a seventeen-year-old male, which she thought was a little surprising, as it was mostly females who tended to attempt suicide by taking pills. Boys tended to use more violent methods. When Alec came in with the teenager, she knew with a sinking sensation this wasn't a typical overdose.

"We found percocet wrappers in his room. We've given him one dose of Narcan on the ride over, but his pupils are still fixed and dilated." Alec's expression was grim, and when she looked down at the boy, she noticed he was built like an athlete. "We intubated him, but he needs a nasogastric tube so he can get activated charcoal."

"How long ago did he take the overdose?" Jillian asked, as she did a quick neuro exam of her own. "Luanne, will you please get me an NG tube?"

"I don't know," Alec said. "I think it was a couple of hours."

A couple of hours wasn't good news. Luanne swiftly

handed over the nasogastric tube and Jillian pulled on a second set of gloves before preparing to insert it.

She managed to get the tube halfway down, but then her fingers seemed to stop working. She fumbled, trying to use her left hand to advance the tube, but Alec was there, reaching over to help her. Between them they managed to get the tube down and in moments Luanne had given the first dose of charcoal.

"Thanks," Jillian murmured. There wasn't time for her to say anything more because her attention was needed for the patient.

"I have the results of his drug screen," Will announced. "Positive for codeine."

Percocets had codeine in them, so at least they knew for certain what he'd taken. Was this an accidental overdose, then? The boy still wasn't waking up and that was more concerning than anything else.

It wasn't until she was unable to squeeze the ambu-bag to give the boy deep breaths as they wheeled him up to the ICU, being forced to let the respiratory therapist take over the task, that Jillian realized her hand was much worse than before.

Her evoked potential tests may have been negative, but there was still something wrong. And deep down she couldn't help but think it was serious.

Maybe she shouldn't go with Alec to his parents' house this weekend. Not until she knew for sure what was wrong with her. She never should have gotten so involved with Alec and his daughter. Shelby had already confided in her, had clung to her when she'd been sick. If she continued to see Alec and Shelby, the little girl might begin to view her as very much of a mother figure.

She might already see Jillian like that already.

Her stomach twisted at the knowledge. After the way Shelby had lost her mother to a non-curable illness, she couldn't bear the thought of putting the little girl through such heartfelt bereavement all over again.

CHAPTER TWELVE

DURING the rest of her shift, Jillian tried not to think about Alec and Shelby. But concentrating on work wasn't helping either. The whole ED was upset about the boy, Derek McNeil, who'd overdosed on percocets. His neurological status had been bad, making his prognosis grim. She really hoped Alec hadn't found him too late.

Frank, her other patient, was still holding his own. So far the hypothermia treatments seemed to be working.

Alec had to leave right after she'd transferred Derek to the ICU so she didn't get a chance to talk to him about how he'd found the boy. Or anything else, like changing her mind about his invitation. Her stomach twisted, making her feel sick.

Thinking about Derek was almost better then dwelling on her health. The idea of a debilitating illness wouldn't leave her. Sitting in her office at the end of her shift, she stared at her hands.

No way around it, she'd have to get in touch with Dr. Juran again, and soon. It was Friday night, though, so she'd have to wait until Monday. The weekend stretched long and empty before her, especially now that she'd decided not to go to Alec's parents' house.

Her pager went off and she looked at the number with a sense of dread. Alec. What could she say to him? She wished she could tell him the truth. Knowing Alec, he'd come right over, take her into his arms and tell her everything would be all right.

If only she could really believe that.

Swallowing against the lump in her throat, she picked up her phone and dialed his number.

"Alec? This is Jillian."

"Are you still at work?" He sounded surprised.

"Yes." Her vision blurred and she forced herself to continue, "I'm sorry, but I won't be able to get away for a while yet."

"I understand, although I was hoping to see you tonight." He sounded disappointed and she hadn't even told him about the weekend yet. "I need to go home, though, to check on Shelby. I called Meagan earlier, and she said Shelby was doing all right, but I want to see her for myself."

"Of course you do." She bit her lip and blinked away the tears. "I'll talk to you later, Alec. Give Shelby a hug for me."

"I will. Jillian, I, uh…" He stopped, sighed and then said, "Never mind. I'll talk to you tomorrow."

"Goodbye, Alec." She quickly hung up the phone before she started sobbing in earnest. Taking several deep breaths, she fought off the feeling of depression and stood. Derek McNeil. She needed to focus on something besides her own misery. Derek's life was on the line, she wanted to go up to the ICU to check on him.

Anything was better than going home to her empty house. Alone.

* * *

Alec stared down at his sleeping daughter, relieved when it seemed she really was better. According to Meagan, her fever had broken about eight o'clock and she hadn't thrown up any more since he'd left for work. By morning, Shelby would no doubt be back to her old self, wide awake and raring to go.

His smile faded. Shelby would be fine, but he couldn't say the same about Derek. Too bad he hadn't found him sooner. Actually, in some ways it was a miracle he'd found the kid at all. He and Rafe had sensed a change in some of the football players' attitudes since the news of Frank's hospitalization had hit the streets. They'd discovered Derek was the unofficial captain of the team, the one who scheduled group weight-training sessions and held study hours for anyone having trouble with the plays. Derek was not just the quarterback of the team but, according to the rest of the players, he was the heart and soul of the team.

They'd thought for sure Derek would tell them the truth behind the percocets.

Instead, they'd found him unconscious, having accidentally overdosed on them.

His mother had sworn the boy wasn't depressed. There was no suicide note, and his mother claimed Derek was thrilled to be the first-string quarterback. He was really hoping for a college scholarship next year and his mother seemed to think there was a good chance he'd get it.

But not any more. Even if Derek woke up from his drug overdose, he'd likely not play any time soon.

This whole thing was far out of control. The kid had almost died, could still die, just because someone was greedy enough to prey on a player's willingness to do anything to be noticed. He'd never seen anything like it. Drugs in any form, narcotics or steroids, were bad news.

At first Derek's mother had insisted they couldn't talk to her son, then she'd finally agreed. She'd thought Derek had been sleeping until she hadn't been able to wake him up. Alec had called 911 and had given basic aid to the boy until the ambulance had got there.

The empty percocet wrappers they'd found had been buried in the bottom of the kid's garbage can. When he'd asked Derek's mother about them, she'd been shocked to know her son had been taking pain pills, although she had admitted Derek had a bad shoulder, his throwing arm no less. She hadn't thought the injury too bad as he'd continued to play. Obviously, Derek had tried to kill the pain in his shoulder.

Stupid. Because he'd almost killed himself instead.

Alec turned away from his sleeping daughter, still seeing Derek in his mind. He'd requested the paramedic give the boy Narcan, the antidote to narcotics, but it hadn't worked. Because Derek had been too far gone? He wasn't sure and could only hope the charcoal had been able to do some good.

The thought of charcoal reminded him of Jillian. Her fingers seemed to be bothering her again. He'd noticed how she'd had difficulty placing the tube, so he'd given her a hand. Thank heavens for his medic training. Placing naso-gastric tubes wasn't hard. He'd had to do far worse when he'd been in the army.

Alec sank into his sofa, scrubbing his palms over his eyes. Derek's face, all the faces of the kids he'd lost, swam through his mind. He'd thought as a police officer in the civilian world he'd have a chance to help people, but most of the time he felt like he was only getting further behind. First there had been Ricky, who'd died of a gunshot wound. Then Frank had ended up in the ICU. Now Derek.

His goal had been to make the world a safer place to live, especially for kids. He felt even more strongly about his mission now that he had Shelby.

He stared at his silent TV, wishing Jillian was there with him. Should he call her again? Maybe she wouldn't mind coming over but leaving before Shelby woke up in the morning.

No, he couldn't be such a jerk. Jillian deserved better than to sneak out of his bedroom at some ridiculously early hour. What would Shelby think if she found Jillian here in the morning? With his bad luck, his daughter would come bouncing into his bedroom early in the morning to find Jillian. Naked.

No way. The vision clinched it. There was no way he could call Jillian this late. She'd sounded odd on the phone earlier, anyway. Was she worried about her hand? She'd told him the tests were negative, but obviously something was wrong.

He fought the urge to call her again.

Tomorrow, he decided, was plenty of time to see Jillian. Maybe at his parents'. Shelby would be busy playing with Bethany so he might be able to find some time alone to talk to Jillian.

At least, he hoped so.

Alec dragged himself upright and made his way to his bedroom, alone.

But he couldn't sleep, because the sheets on his bed carried Jillian's sultry scent.

The next morning, Shelby woke him up by bouncing on his bed. He'd been dreaming of Jillian, fantastic dreams, reliving those moments they'd made love. For a moment he'd experienced a rare urge to bury his head under his pillow until his daughter got the hint and left him alone. Immediately ashamed of himself, Alec roused himself from his bed, flashing Shelby a big grin.

"What would you like for breakfast this morning?" he asked, willing his mind to block the images of his X-rated dreams.

"Daisy and I want to go for a walk in the park," Shelby announced. "You promised."

His daughter sure liked to use his words against him, didn't she? Stifling a sigh, he headed for the kitchen. "And we will go the park, after breakfast."

"Now, Daddy." Shelby planted her hands on her slim hips, her lower lip thrust forward.

There was no way he was going to the park until he'd had something to eat and showered. He wasn't willing to see Jillian while looking like a slug. "Shelby," he said, his tone warning he was serious, "we're going to eat breakfast. Do you want cereal or eggs?"

Shelby flashed a mutinous glare and he was struck by how much she reminded him of himself at her age. With a wry grin, he realized his parents were true saints for raising six kids, most of them boys. For all the trouble he'd gotten into as a kid, he could really appreciate the good side of growing up in a large family.

He wanted the same thing for his kids.

When his daughter didn't answer right away, he made the decision for her by going to the fridge for eggs. After a few minutes Shelby flopped into a chair, her chin practically dragging on her chest as he whipped up a batch of scrambled eggs and toast.

Her attitude had mellowed by the time he set a plate in front of her and she dug into the food with enthusiasm. When she'd finished, her expression was hopeful. "Now can we go to the park, Daddy?"

"As soon as I shower," he promised, carrying his dirty dishes to the sink. "And don't say it," he warned, lifting his hand to stop her when she opened her mouth. "You need to learn a little patience, Shelby. It only takes me fifteen minutes to shower and shave. Surely you can wait that long?"

"I guess," she said with a long-suffering sigh, as if he'd asked her to wait fifteen hours instead. "But will you at least hurry?"

Alec rolled his eyes and headed for the bathroom. Despite what he'd said, he actually did hurry, which was ridiculous, considering he'd just lectured his daughter on the merits of patience. Yet he couldn't deny he was anxious to see Jillian again.

Shelby waited for him, Daisy already clipped to her leash by the time he'd emerged from his room, dressed in soft denim jeans and a blue and gray striped polo shirt. The barbeque at his parents didn't start until two, so they had plenty of time. He and Shelby walked Daisy around the park, laughing when the dog tried to chase the birds.

It was close to ten-thirty in the morning before they'd made their way over to the side of the park closest to

Jillian's house. Even though Alec knew he'd see Jillian later, he walked up to the front door and knocked.

He frowned when no one came to the door. He knocked again, louder, in case Jillian hadn't heard him, but after a few minutes he swallowed his disappointment and drew Shelby away.

"She's probably still sleeping—we'll see her later," Alec said in a cheerful voice. Jillian had worked late the night before, she was no doubt tired. "Come on, I'll race you home."

Shelby let out a shriek and took off at a run, Daisy's short legs galloping madly in an effort to keep up. Alec slowed down to let Shelby win the race as they neared home.

He waited until noon to call Jillian. When the answering-machine kicked on, he left a quick message, asking Jillian to call him back. Then he paged her.

Pacing the length of the kitchen, he battled despair when she didn't immediately answer. What had happened? Was she still sleeping? Or had she changed her mind about going? It wasn't as if this was the first time she'd meet his family— the whole clan had been there for Shelby's birthday.

When his phone rang he was so startled he jumped from his chair, causing it to topple over behind him. "Hello?"

"Alec? It's Jillian." Her voice sounded nasal, stuffed up as if she had a bad cold. "I'm sorry, but I'm not feeling very well. I don't think I can make it today after all."

He ignored the sharp piercing disappointment. "You sound awful. Is there anything I can do? Shelby and I could bring over some chicken soup," he offered.

She sniffled loudly and for a moment it sounded as if she were crying. "No, I don't want either of you to get sick, but thanks for the offer. I'm sorry, Alec. Hopefully I'll be better in a few days."

"I hope so, too. Take care of yourself," he told her, realizing that she really did sound sick. First Shelby had come down with flu, now Jillian had a cold. He should be grateful he was feeling fine, but he knew if it were only him, he'd take the risk and go to Jillian.

Dejected, he hung up the phone. "Jillian is sick, Shelby, so you and I are on our own for the barbeque."

"Aw." Shelby looked as disappointed as he felt. "That's OK, Daddy. We'll have fun anyway, right? I'll keep you company so you're not lonely."

Her words stunned him. Did Shelby realize how important Jillian was to him? He wouldn't be surprised if she did. His young daughter was amazingly astute, especially when it came to reading others' feelings. Reaching down, he drew her in for a quick hug.

"I love you, Shelby," he said in a husky tone. "And don't worry about me. I'm not lonely now that I have you. You and I will be just fine together."

"Yep," Shelby readily agreed. "Because we're a team, right, Daddy?"

"Right."

But later that day, while he was truly enjoying himself at his parents' barbeque, he couldn't help the pang of regret when Abby asked where Jillian was.

Because even though he loved his daughter, there was a tiny part of him that did long for something more than just being a parent.

Shelby was important, his daughter meant the world to him, but suddenly Jillian did, too.

Now that he'd had a taste of what it would be like to have a family, a true partnership like his parents had, he wouldn't be completely satisfied with anything less.

He wanted that family and partnership with Jillian.

Jillian buried her head in her pillow, stifling her uncontrollable sobs the best she could. Despair filled her heart all the way down to her soul, grieving for something she couldn't have.

After several long minutes she managed to get herself under control. Although she'd been fighting this battle all day, going through crying jags since earlier that morning, once she'd gotten off the phone with Dr. Juran.

Her symptoms hadn't gone away overnight and when she'd gotten up, the thought of waiting until Monday to talk to Dr. Juran had seemed impossible. So she'd paged the neurology specialist through the hospital operator, not sure if he wore his pager even when he wasn't on call.

He did. He'd called her back and listened as she'd described how the symptoms were worse. How she couldn't squeeze an ambu-bag to breathe for a patient, neither could she place a nasogastric tube.

"Your new assistant called to tell me the evoked potential tests were negative, so what in the world is wrong with me?" she'd asked in agonizing frustration.

There had been a long silence and her stomach had clenched painfully.

"I'm sorry, Jillian, but my new assistant got the test results mixed up. Your evoked potential tests weren't negative."

Dear Lord. "They weren't?" she'd said in a tiny voice.

"No. I don't like to give this sort of information over the

phone, but I'm afraid you are in the very early stages of multiple sclerosis. The good news is that your symptoms are mild and there's a new medication regime with excellent results just been approved by the FDA. You have many treatment options, Jillian. I have no doubt you'll practice medicine for many years yet."

She couldn't even recall what she'd said to him, had no doubt promised to make an appointment in the clinic to see him, before hanging up the phone and bursting into tears.

To make matters worse, she'd lied to Alec.

She didn't have a cold. She was sick to a certain degree, sick at heart. Because she knew the right thing to do was to break off her relationship with Alec now, before it was too late, for Shelby's sake.

Her eyes filled with tears again as she imagined Alec and Shelby at his parents' barbeque.

Who was she kidding? It was already too late.

She loved him. Loved being a part of his and Shelby's life. But she couldn't imagine Alec really understood what it was like to share their life with someone who was only going to get weaker, to the point where she'd be dependent on them to help her get out of bed to the bathroom.

She squeezed her eyes shut, imagining Alec's jade-green eyes filled with pity. Imagining Shelby's distress.

No, she couldn't do it.

She refused to become a burden to the ones she loved.

CHAPTER THIRTEEN

JILLIAN dodged Alec's phone calls over the rest of the weekend, but each time she did, she realized she couldn't keep avoiding him for ever. For one thing, he lived too close, just on the other side of the park. For another, he was too stubborn to give up without seeing her in person. She half expected him to show up on her doorstep again, but he didn't.

At least, not yet. But it was only a matter of time.

While it hadn't been easy, she'd used the weekend to pull herself together. She'd grieved for the family she might have had with Alec, but finally managed to stop crying long enough to focus on her future. She refused to walk around in a state of constant depression. Her life wasn't over, not by a long shot. In fact, the more she'd thought about it over the weekend, the more she'd realized maybe it was time to consider a career change.

She loved the variety of emergency medicine, but maybe she should specialize in neurology instead. The idea of dedicating her life to research benefiting MS made her feel as if she might have some control over her illness. After searching various Web sites to gather information on multiple sclerosis, she grew even more impressed with the various treatment options that were indeed available. Dr. Juran hadn't been kidding when he'd mentioned the new medication regime. The stories of people who'd overcome their MS symptoms, to do fifty-mile bike rides or to compete in sprint triathlons, were amazing.

If they could do it, she could, too. All she needed to do was to make up her mind to remain positive.

Which was easier to do if she didn't think about losing Alec. And Shelby.

She dragged herself out of bed earlier than usual on Monday morning, hoping to do her three-mile run in the park without seeing Alec and Shelby. Eight o'clock wasn't exactly early, unless you took into account that her body was accustomed to second-shift hours.

She made it to the last mile when she saw Alec and Shelby come out of their house, Daisy in tow. They saw her at the same moment and Shelby broke away from her father's side, dashing toward her with Daisy barking excitedly at her heels.

"Jillian!" she called. "Wait up! We want to walk with you."

She bit down on her lower lip, hoping she could do this without breaking down. "Call you later, Shelby, after I finish my run." Without slowing her pace at all, Jillian kept right on going.

The flash of hurt in Shelby's gaze tore at her, and she stumbled, almost giving in to the need to stop and beg for forgiveness. Hardening her heart, knowing the pain Shelby felt now would be far less than if she dragged this on longer, Jillian lengthened her stride and ran the rest of the way home.

As she got out of the shower, she heard the phone ring and instinctively knew the caller was Alec, even before she heard his deep voice on her answering-machine.

"Jillian, call me when you get this message. I tried to explain to Shelby why you wanted to finish your run this morning, but I'm afraid her feelings are hurt. Maybe we can have a picnic in the park before work, so Shelby knows your brush-off wasn't personal." There was the slightest bit of accusation underlying his tone.

Not that she blamed him.

With a trembling finger, she erased the message without calling him back.

"Daddy, I don't think Jillian likes us any more."

The expression of utter dejection in his daughter's face rekindled the simmering anger Alec felt toward Jillian.

She hadn't called him back. She was avoiding him and avoiding Shelby. And he didn't know why.

If he hadn't seen Jillian's brush-off with his own eyes, he wouldn't have believed it. It was one thing to give him the cold shoulder, but to be so cruel to a seven-year-old, especially one who'd put her on a pedestal, was unforgivable.

"Hey, munchkin, don't worry about Jillian. I think she's just really busy right now. We're having fun without her, aren't we?"

"I guess." Shelby's less than enthusiastic response as she idly plucked blades of grass wasn't reassuring. Her tiny brow was furrowed in a frown as she glanced up at him. "Did you do something to make her mad, Daddy?"

Not that he knew of. If anyone had the right to be mad it was him. This was why he hadn't wanted to get involved in a relationship. Poor Shelby had been through so much she didn't need to be hurt like this. He could ignore his own pain, but not Shelby's.

"Sweetheart, let's not worry about Jillian." He reached over to take Shelby's hand in his. "We're a father-daughter team, aren't we?"

A reluctant smile curved her lips. "Right." Just then the dog climbed into her lap and licked her chin, making her laugh. "But don't forget Daisy. She's part of our team, too."

"Absolutely. I'd never forget Daisy," Alec agreed. The conversation moved on to school, shopping and Bethany's birthday party coming up in a few weeks, but even though he was relieved to see Shelby smile, he silently vowed to see Jillian in person, to figure out the motive behind her behavior.

As he dressed in his uniform for work, he stared at his bed and remembered the way Jillian had looked as he'd taken her scrubs off at the same time she'd unbuttoned his shirt. She was so beautiful. Aside from finding Shelby, making love to Jillian had been the best thing to happen to him in a long time, although the experience couldn't have affected her nearly as much. That she could simply turn her back on him and his daughter was incomprehensible.

Turning his back on the bed, he resolutely clipped his handcuffs into the holder on his belt and shoved memories of Jillian aside. He and Rafe were heading out to arrest a kid by the name of Nelson Daniels. So far, the few players who had come forward had named this Nelson Daniels as the supplier of the percocets. Which was odd because, from what he and Rafe could tell, Nelson didn't have a contact inside the hospital.

The drugs had to be coming from someone with access inside the hospital, which narrowed their list down to Eric Graves, Luanne's younger brother, or Jerry Green, Susan's son. Both nurses' names were at the top of their suspect list.

They were recorded by the machine often, but so far the camera hadn't picked up either one of them shoving the medication into their pockets.

Although since the camera had been put in place, there hadn't been any narcotic discrepancies either.

Still, his gut told him they were on the right track. If all went well, he'd have this case closed by the end of his shift.

Thank heavens he could occupy his mind with something other than Jillian's betrayal.

"Daddy?" Shelby asked as he prepared to leave.

"Yes?" He turned to his daughter.

She rushed over to him. "I need a hug."

He lifted Shelby into his arms, his throat thick with emotion as she clung to him. He held her close for a long minute, smoothing a hand down her shiny brown hair. "Hey, what's the matter, munchkin?"

"Nothing," she mumbled against his shoulder. "I love you, Daddy."

"I love you, too, Shelby." He put her down with regret. A week ago he'd talked to Shelby about his job and she'd seemed fine afterwards. Obviously, his daughter was still upset over Jillian. He wished he could stay home with her, but he couldn't. "I'll see you in the morning, OK?"

She nodded, her expression solemn. "Be careful, Daddy."

"I will." He left the house, waving at Shelby as she watched him from the doorway. It wasn't until he'd radioed in and made arrangements to meet Rafe to review the final elements of their trap that his brain registered just how worried Shelby had seemed.

Maybe she wasn't as OK with his job as he'd thought.

The comments Jillian had made about changing his career for Shelby's sake came back in a rush. As much as he tried, he couldn't erase the image of his daughter's face peering at him from the doorway.

Jillian drove to work, hoping the ED would be busy enough to keep her mind occupied. Because despite her best efforts, Alec's accusing voice slipped into her subconscious so that she heard his words over and over again.

Shelby's feelings were hurt. Call me. Shelby's feelings were hurt. Hurt. Hurt. It wasn't personal…

But it was. Very personal.

She sighed, knowing she needed to talk to Alec face to face. To let him know why their relationship was over. He might not understand, but eventually, hopefully, he'd learn to forgive her.

And to forget?

The idea of Alec finding someone else to share his life caused a rare surge of jealousy to clench in her belly.

Of course he deserved to share his life with someone. To have a family, more children, with a woman who could be a true partner in every way.

Too bad she couldn't be that person.

Jillian headed into the ED with a determined stride. Here at least, amidst the chaos, she was comfortable. In charge.

After locking her purse in her office, she headed into the arena, her attention centered on the whiteboard, with the full listing of patients.

Someone bumped into her from behind. She turned, catching a glimpse of Luanne.

"Sorry, Jillian," Luanne murmured.

"Are you OK, Lu?" Jillian frowned. Luanne looked as if she'd been crying.

"Derek died this morning."

Derek had died. Jillian closed her eyes on a wave of pain. No wonder Luanne was upset.

"I have to go," Luanne continued, half-dazed. "I can't— I have to leave."

"Take care, Luanne. Talk to you tomorrow."

"Bye." Luanne ducked her head and quickly walked toward the staff locker room.

Obviously Luanne, along with everyone else in the ED, was still on edge, although it had been days since the last narcotic theft. Jillian glanced over, nearly groaning when she saw Wayne coming toward her.

"We have a full house. Do you think you can handle it?" he asked. "Or do you want me to stay?"

She'd rather work alone than with Wayne so she shook her head. "I'll be fine. Any patients in particular I need to know about?"

"All of them, I assume." He turned to the board and quickly ran down the entire list of patients, telling her exactly what needed to be done. The man had the personality of a toad, but he obviously knew his stuff as far as emergency medicine was concerned.

"Thanks," she said when he'd finished.

He turned to leave. Amy, the charge nurse, who'd switched shifts with Luanne, stood by the narcotic dispensing machine and called her name. "Dr. Davis?"

"Yes? What is it?" With a sinking feeling, Jillian hurried over.

"Eighteen percocets are missing." Amy's face was red

as she met Jillian's gaze. "And you're listed as the person who removed them."

"What?" How could that be? She'd only been in the ED for a measly half-hour. She reached over and snatched from Amy's fingers the narcotic discrepancy notice generated by the machine. "Let me see that."

There it was, in clear bold print, her name and the starting percocet count of eighteen, yet the final count was zero.

"I don't understand," she whispered. The time of the transaction was listed as three-fifteen and it was three-thirty now. "I haven't even been inside the narcotic dispensing machine yet today. I just got here. I've been getting report from Dr. Netter."

"Is there a problem?" Wayne sauntered over and for a brief moment she wondered if he'd done this to her, framing her for the thefts just to discredit her and take over the role of medical director.

"Yes, there's a problem. Someone used my password to take percocets from the machine." Jillian tried to keep up a brave front, but the way Amy skirted her gaze didn't help. How could this have happened? Then she recalled Alec telling her he could see her enter in her password that day. She had since changed it and had been more careful, but it seemed she hadn't been careful enough. Her heart sank.

"I have to report this," Amy said, reaching for the phone.

Glued to the spot, Jillian couldn't move. Not even when Amy hung up, telling her Rose Jenkins and the director of security were on the way. Not even when Chris arrived, his bushy eyebrows pulled together in a deep frown.

After she'd been questioned for almost an hour, and her office and car searched, they still didn't look convinced.

They hadn't found anything, but her relief was short-lived.

Chris stepped forward. "Jillian, I think we should suspend you from duty while we investigate this situation."

"Why? We know this person has been stealing passwords." She glanced at the somber faces of the hospital administrators surrounding her. "Do you want me to give you a urine sample so you can test for drugs? Because I will."

"That would help," her boss admitted. "Jillian, I'm sure you understand our position. We'll need to inform the police and let them take it from here, and I think it would be better for everyone if you take a few days off." Chris turned to where Wayne hovered on the outskirts of the group, blatantly listening as he pretended to help cover patients. "Wayne, will you assume the role of interim medical director? I also need you to cover Jillian's shift."

"Of course." Wayne didn't go as far as to smile, but the light in his eyes was gleeful enough. "Don't worry about a thing."

Jillian didn't speak, couldn't think of anything to say in her defense. Submitting to the humiliating process of giving a urine sample was the worst. Once she'd finished, the two male security guards who'd searched her desk and her car accompanied her along the entire route back to the ED.

"I need to get my purse out of my office," she said in a low voice.

The two security guards hovered in the doorway. Jillian stood there for a moment, wondering what would happen to her. Where could she go? What could she do? As much as she wanted to call Alec, she shied away from that idea, knowing he wouldn't be thrilled to hear from her.

The security guards sent her sidelong curious looks.

Did they think she was going to go off the deep end, do something completely irrational?

They didn't find the percocets because she didn't have them. Someone else did.

Being alone had never been so hard. She needed someone to talk to. Alec. She wished more than anything she could talk to Alec. But she couldn't. Luanne? Yes, Luanne was a good friend. She'd understand. Grabbing her purse and her keys, she headed for the door. She'd been to Luanne's house a few times. Thank heavens she didn't live far.

And maybe Luanne would remember if there had been anyone else around the narcotic dispensing machine.

Jillian didn't remember much about the drive to Luanne's house. When she arrived, she noticed Luanne lugging a suitcase to her car parked in the driveway.

"Lu, do you have a minute? I really need to talk."

Luanne's eyes darted to the street behind her. "Ah, I'm sorry, but you caught us as we were getting ready to leave. My brother and I are going out of town."

They were? In the middle of the week? "Just a few minutes? Please? This time it was my password used to steal narcotics."

Instead of being shocked, Luanne tossed the suitcase into the back seat and shut the door. "Don't worry, you have an excellent reputation, Jillian. There isn't a single person there who will believe you're taking drugs."

"What? Luanne, this is serious."

"I know." Luanne's eyes filled with tears. "I can't talk about this now. You don't understand. I have to go. I have to take Eric and go."

As Luanne became more and more agitated, Jillian

realized the truth. Seconds later a police car pulled up in front of the house, with Alec and Rafe inside.

Luanne was the one who'd taken the drugs.

CHAPTER FOURTEEN

ALEC couldn't believe Jillian was there, talking to Luanne. He tried to tell her with his eyes to get out of the way, but she stood there, next to Luanne, as if her feet had been fused to the cement.

"Luanne, it's over." Alec tried to keep his tone non-threatening, especially the way Luanne looked as if she might bolt. "We've arrested Nelson Daniels and he told us he obtained the percocets from your brother Eric. Our hidden camera caught you slipping the percocets into your pocket just a couple of hours ago. It's all over."

To his surprise, Jillian rounded on him. "Look, there must be something we can do. I'm sure there's a reasonable explanation for Luanne's behavior."

"Jillian's right." Luanne's eyes filled with tears. "Eric didn't want to give Nelson the drugs. Nelson blackmailed him. He threatened to hurt Eric if he didn't co-operate."

Alec could see how that might happen. "Nelson was blackmailing you into getting the drugs?" He tried to maneuver around Jillian to get her out of the way, but she wasn't co-operating.

"He stole them from Eric the first time." Luanne crossed

her arms over her chest as if she were cold. It seemed that once she started talking, she couldn't stop. "I took them for Eric, without paying for them, because he was injured." Her eyes flicked to Jillian's, pleading for understanding. "Our mother just lost her job and we were broke. I wanted to help Eric get a scholarship. Nelson threatened to get us all into trouble if he didn't get more. I didn't know what to do. Eric is one of the best players on the team." Her shoulders slumped. "I just didn't know what to do.

"It's OK, Luanne." Jillian tried to go to her friend, but Alec grabbed her arm. In his eyes, Luanne was still a suspect. He didn't want Jillian to get in the way of the arrest. "I swear, we can find a way out of this. I'll help you."

Tears spilled down Luanne's cheeks. "I'm sorry I framed you, Jillian. I just needed time to get away. When Derek died, I knew I couldn't do this any more. I figured no one would seriously believe you were guilty. I just couldn't find a way out."

Alec felt sorry for Luanne, but he couldn't let that stop him from taking her in. He hadn't known about Jillian being framed for the theft. True to form, Jillian was being kind, which made arresting Luanne in front of her even harder.

Rafe stepped around them and approached Luanne, taking her wrists and placing the handcuffs on before she could move away. "You'll need to come down to the station with us. I'm sure if you co-operate, the judge will go easier on you."

A movement caught Alec's attention and he noticed Eric had rounded the corner of the house and was walking toward them. Jillian pulled out of his grasp and Alec took his eyes off the kid for a brief moment, worried she'd get in the way.

"Stay back!" Dammit, he wished she wasn't there.

"Let my sister go!" Eric shouted. When Alec glanced back at him, he saw the kid was holding a gun. Seeing his sister in handcuffs must have pushed him over the edge.

Alec could have reached for his own weapon, but didn't. Taking a slow breath, he kept his hands up where the kid could see them. "The violence stops here, Eric. Don't make this worse than it needs to be. We'll let your sister go if you drop the gun."

"What are you doing, Eric?" Luanne called out, sobbing. "Stop it. Put the gun down."

"You heard her," Alec repeated, trying to edge closer to the boy. "Put the gun down, Eric. No one needs to get hurt."

"It's over," Luanne told him. Eric stared at her as if unsure what to do. "It's over," she repeated.

"I don't want to go to jail." Slowly, he raised the gun but the barrel was turned toward his temple. Alec knew the boy was going to pull the trigger.

"No!" Alec rushed forward, grabbing the gun and trying to pull it away from the teen's head. They wrestled for a moment, and the gun went off, two shots in rapid succession.

A flash of neon blue pain blinded him, blazing a fiery path through his body. His last conscious thought was of his daughter.

Shelby.

Jillian watched the events unfold in slow motion. When the sound of gunfire split the air, she froze, unable to believe Alec had been hurt.

But then his body went limp, falling to the ground.

"Alec!" Hardly realizing she was screaming his name,

she rushed forward. In some corner of her mind she heard Eric crying in the background and Rafe calling on his radio for help, something about an officer down, but her gaze was fixed on Alec's still features.

Rolling Alec on his back, she ripped his uniform shirt open, searching for wounds. Instead of finding flesh and blood, lots of blood, she found the surface of a Kevlar vest.

For a moment she closed her eyes in relief. But if he was wearing a bulletproof vest, why was he still unconscious? Had the bullet managed to penetrate the Kevlar? She felt along the thick material, feeling a bullet imbedded halfway into the vest.

She knew the force of being shot in the chest at close range could be enough to stop a man's heart, so she checked his pulse. It was there, faint and too fast. Intent on taking the vest off so she could examine the skin underneath, she loosened his belt only to notice a strange, dark stain on his uniform, high on his thigh. With a sinking feeling, she touched the stain and looked down at her fingertips.

Blood.

Dear God. He'd been hit below the vest.

She fumbled with the rest of his clothes, exposing the wound so she could assess the damage. At the rate blood was pouring from his groin, she knew his femoral artery had been hit.

She folded up Alec's uniform shirt and pressed it over the seeping wound, leaning on her hands with all her weight to help slow the blood loss.

"The paramedics are on the way," Rafe murmured. She glanced up at him, noting how he'd gotten both Luanne and Eric in handcuffs. She felt bad for Luanne, but her attention was riveted on Alec, who was losing blood at a brisk pace.

Hang in there, Alec, she silently begged as she waited impatiently for the paramedic unit to arrive. Alec needed blood and fluids as soon as humanly possible.

And if they were to save his leg, he'd need surgery as well.

But there was nothing Jillian could do without help. Without supplies. She'd never felt more helpless in her entire life.

Don't die, Alec. Shelby needs you. I need you. Don't die. Please, don't die…

When the paramedic unit finally arrived, Jillian continued to hold pressure as the paramedics started IVs in both of Alec's antecubital veins. Once they had intubated him to protect his airway and hung fluids wide open on both IVs, they looked at the wound under his vest. Luckily, Jillian could see the skin was bruised, but nothing had penetrated his chest. Then they asked her to let up on the groin wound so they could examine the arterial bleed.

Throughout the interminable waiting, Jillian let up on the pressure every five minutes to help encourage some perfusion of Alec's leg. Saving his life was the first priority, but if there was also a way to save his leg, she intended to do it.

The older paramedic wanted to use a mechanical pressure device, but Jillian didn't agree. "Manual pressure is better. And it's easier with manual pressure to remember to let up on the pressure long enough to perfuse his leg."

When the guy looked as if he might argue again, she shook her head and glared at him. "No. As the doctor I'm giving you an order for manual pressure. I'll hold it myself all the way to Trinity Medical Center if I have to."

"All right." The paramedics exchanged a surprised look,

but left her alone after that. She did hold pressure on Alec's wound throughout the ambulance ride. Staring down at Alec's still facial features was the hardest thing she'd ever had to do.

"Call ahead, tell them to have a vascular surgeon available when we get there," she instructed the paramedic.

He nodded his head and made the call.

What else could she do? Nothing. His heart was surprisingly stable, although she'd noticed a few irregular beats. Fluids and transporting him to the hospital as quickly as possible were the priorities.

She remembered that night—had it only been three weeks ago?—when Alec had done the same thing, held manual pressure over their John Doe's bleeding chest wound. She'd been surprised Alec had taken the boy's death so hard. He seemed to take his job very seriously, almost to the extreme of doing whatever necessary to save a life.

Tonight, grabbing for Eric's gun had been risky. He'd saved the boy's life, but at the possible expense of his own.

The screaming siren echoed in her head as the ambulance rushed to Trinity Medical Center. As soon as the ambulance stopped, the second paramedic flung the back doors open and prepared to move Alec inside.

Perched on the edge of the gurney, Jillian kept her balance as the paramedics slid Alec out of the ambulance and inside the ED. She knew Wayne would be surprised to see her, but she didn't care. No matter what she felt towards Wayne on a personal basis, he was a good doctor.

"Is the vascular surgeon here?" Jillian asked.

"Right here." The vascular surgeon, Dr. Travis Smythe, stepped forward. "What do you have?"

"Femoral artery bleed. He's lost several units of blood."

Wayne snapped out orders for O-negative blood to be given through the rapid infuser. When Dr. Smythe told her to let up on the wound, she did.

"We'll take him directly to the OR," he said after three seconds of watching the blood well at an amazing pace. "Draw a full panel of labs and get ready to move."

Will Patterson was already filling numerous tubes of blood. In moments he slapped labels on them and sent them to the lab for testing. Jillian placed her hands back over the wound to apply pressure.

It was almost another ten minutes, which seemed like hours, before they wheeled Alec up to the OR suites for surgery. Jillian let up on the pressure, awkwardly jumped down from the gurney and stepped back to let the surgical team take over.

She wanted to stay. If she put up enough of a ruckus, they'd probably let her. But she turned away, knowing it was best if she let the experts do their job. Travis Smythe was a good surgeon. If anyone could save Alec's leg and his life, Travis could.

After washing Alec's blood off her hands, Jillian headed back down to the waiting room in the ED. When she walked in, she saw Alec's parents, Shelby, Alaina and Abby, along with his future brother-in-law, Nick.

When Shelby saw Jillian she broke free of Abby's embrace and rushed toward Jillian, sobbing. Jillian caught the little girl close and hugged her hard.

"I'm sorry, Shelby. He'll be OK. The surgeon is going to fix his wound. Your dad will be OK."

As Alec's family clustered around her, including her in

their group embrace, crying as they offered silent support, Jillian prayed she was telling the truth.

Hours later, Dr. Smythe came to let them know the operation was over. He was cautiously optimistic that Alec would regain full function of his leg, and that the bruising to his heart wouldn't leave any permanent damage.

Shelby, who had clung to Jillian during the entire time, visibly brightened. "Can I see my daddy?"

"Not just yet," Dr. Smythe said. "Give us a little time to get him settled. He's going to spend the night in the ICU, so we can keep a close watch on his circulation and because I didn't want to take the breathing tube out yet. We should be able to remove it in the morning, though, and if all goes well, he'll transfer out to a regular room by the afternoon."

"Thank heavens," Abby murmured, clutching Nick's hand. She glanced at Alaina and Jillian. "We should take turns staying with him. I can take the first watch if you like."

"Adam will be here soon," Alaina pointed out. "He was called in for an emergency case, but planned to stop here afterwards. He's going to want a turn, too."

The Monroe family was really something, pulling together in a crisis in a way she'd never experienced before.

But falling in love with Alec, with his entire family, didn't change the facts. She couldn't impose her illness on them. And this was exactly why. If she were in a relationship with Alec, his entire family would rally around her in a similar situation. Her multiple sclerosis would affect everyone.

Shelby most of all.

It was time for her to leave.

She waited until Adam arrived, looking harried and concerned, before trying to break away. She didn't get very far, because Shelby caught her.

"Are you still mad at my daddy?" Shelby asked, her eyes red and puffy from crying.

"No, Shelby, I'm not mad at anyone." How could she explain why she needed to leave when she really wanted to stay?

"Jillian?" Abby left Nick's side to come over, a frown furrowed in her brow. "Aren't you going to stay? I'm sure you'll want to see that Alec is all right."

Between Alec's family and the wan expression on Shelby's face, she wavered. She couldn't leave Shelby now. She'd stay, at least until Alec was safely out of the ICU.

But being a part of the close-knit Monroe family for a short time, knowing it couldn't last, would be pure torture.

Rafe showed up, asking about Alec. After he'd gone to see his partner, Jillian walked over to him.

"What will happen to Luanne and Eric?"

"They'll be allowed out on bail until their court case," replied Rafe. "But I can't lie to you, Jillian. Her case is serious now that Derek died."

Jillian closed her eyes, feeling sick. "I wish there was something I could do."

"You might be able to testify on her behalf." Rafe lifted a shoulder. "And she'll need a good lawyer."

Jillian could afford to pay for the lawyer and made up her mind to call one, soon. "Thanks, Rafe, I appreciate you letting me know."

"I'll check on Alec tomorrow," he promised before he left.

The night was long, but no one complained as each of the family members took turns sitting beside Alec's bedside. When it came to Jillian's turn, she clutched his hand and wished things could be different. Wished she was healthy.

By morning, true to Travis's words, they eased off on his sedation and removed the breathing tube. His family was much happier now they could converse with him. Jillian's eyes burned with unshed tears at the way Alec cradled his daughter close, reassuring her.

An hour later, they had transferred Alec to a regular room. Which would have been Jillian's cue to leave, except Alec surprised her by capturing her hand and tugging her closer. "We need to talk," he said in a low tone.

She nodded, knowing he was right. Exhausted from lack of sleep, she downed another cup of coffee as his family said their goodbyes. Poor Shelby was practically falling asleep half-sprawled on Alaina's lap, so they left, promising to return later.

Once the room had emptied, an awkward silence fell. Jillian realized she owed Alec the truth. He deserved that much, although she knew he'd try to talk her out of her decision.

"You were right," he said. At her puzzled expression, he added, "About my career and Shelby. I thought we'd straightened everything out, but after this…" He paused, grimaced then shifted on the bed. "I can't imagine how scared she must have been."

"You were trying to protect her, Alec," Jillian said softly. "But Shelby needs you."

"I know." Alec flashed a lopsided grin. "And I'm going to take your advice about moving to something less dangerous. I've decided to sit for the detective exam," he admitted. "I'm not smart like you, Jillian. I've avoided the detective exam for years because I didn't want to be humiliated if I failed it."

It was on the tip of her tongue to offer to help him, but then realized she wouldn't be around to help him. Not if she ended their relationship. "You're smarter than you give yourself credit for, Alec," she gently chided. "I have no doubt you'll pass the test fine."

He nodded and she suspected his motivation to pass would help him overcome his fears. "During my years in the army, I saw too much death and destruction. Most of the soldiers were young, adolescent kids. I guess I've used that as an excuse to stay a street cop, focusing my energies on saving kids. Maybe just trying to make up for all those needless deaths I saw."

Jillian sucked in a harsh breath, imagining what it must have been like to live through something like that. No wonder he'd given up his army career to move into law enforcement.

No wonder he'd wrestled for Eric's gun.

"And what about you, Jillian?"

She frowned. "What do you mean?"

"It's clear you've been avoiding me. Us. Why?"

There was no point in lying, not after all this. "I have bad news, Alec." Meeting his gaze was difficult. "Dr. Juran told me there was a mix-up and my evoked potential tests were really positive. I have multiple sclerosis."

His eyes darkened. "I'm sorry, Jillian. I'm sure that was a shock for you." He held out a hand, urging her to come over to stand by his bed. Against her better judgment, she placed her hand in his. "What treatment options did he offer? I'll be there for you, Jillian. Whatever they are, we'll face them together."

Face them together? The thought almost made her cry. Standing by his bed, she tried to remain strong. "Alec, you don't understand. My symptoms are mild now, but they're going to get worse. Much worse." He scowled, but she pressed on, anxious to give him the full picture. "By the time my mother died, she couldn't walk. She needed help eating and getting to the bathroom. I think it's better for you and for Shelby if we just go our separate ways."

"Jillian, I love you." His fingers tightened around hers. "Do you think having MS changes how I feel about you?"

Tears blurred her vision and she tried to pull out of his grasp. "Alec, don't. Please."

"Don't what?" he asked in a harsh tone. "Love you? Sorry, Jillian, it's too late for that."

He loved her. He actually loved her!

"And don't give me this rubbish about your illness. Because I know damn well if I'd have lost my leg, you wouldn't have walked away."

"That's different," she protested. "You can be independent with one leg. We're talking about MS, a very debilitating illness."

"It's an excuse to leave." Alec's eyes glittered with a rare anger. "You're not debilitated now, Jillian. And as a doctor, you know there are new medical breakthroughs every day. What if they find a cure for MS five years from now? Are you willing to throw our love away because you're afraid? To throw away the chance to be a family?"

Stunned, she stared at him. Because he was right. She honestly had been using her MS as an excuse to leave.

Hadn't she already convinced herself she had years before she needed to worry? She swallowed hard. "I couldn't bear it if you looked at me with pity, Alec. And Shelby—she's already lost someone once…"

"Jillian, sit down." His voice was soft as he tugged her down beside him on the bed. "You can't live your life thinking like that. You know you can't. I love you. I want to marry you."

"Oh, Alec," she whispered, "I love you, too."

"Thank heavens," he murmured. "You have no idea how much I needed to hear you say that."

She let out a strangled laugh at his blunt honesty. "I love you, Alec," she repeated, louder this time. "I love you, I love Shelby, and I love your family. I really don't want to be a burden to you, but I realize now I was doing the same thing, trying to protect you from the truth."

"And that's not fair to either of us, is it?" He pulled her on top of him, wrapping his arms around her. "We'll fight this together, Jillian. I've learned the hard way the value of family. You can face almost anything if we're together. And I'm really good at fighting the odds and winning."

Together. With Alec's love and the whole Monroe family behind them, she couldn't see how they could possibly fail. "Maybe we'd better ask Shelby how she feels about this."

Alec lowered his head to kiss her. "Shelby loves you," he murmured against her lips. "But more importantly, Shelby wants me to be happy. And marrying you, Jillian, will make me the happiest guy in the world."

Well, then. How could she argue with that?

EPILOGUE

ABBY and Nick's wedding was elegant and beautiful.

As the best man, Alec stood beside Nick, devastatingly handsome in a black tux. Alaina was the matron of honor and Shelby was gorgeous in her rose-colored flower-girl dress. Jillian had to laugh because almost the entire wedding party was made up of Monroes.

Her heart swelled as Nick and Abby solemnly exchanged vows. She and Alec had announced their engagement weeks ago but hadn't wanted to infringe on Abby's wedding by telling their own intention to get married sooner, rather than later.

Alec's impatience made her laugh. He'd made it clear he wasn't willing to wait over a year, like Abby and Nick had, to make her his wife. Months were too long. If he had his way, they'd be married within the week.

As the minister announced the newly married couple, Jillian clapped as loudly as the rest of the guests in church. After Dr. Juran had started her on medication, the numbness and tingling in her hands had disappeared.

She knew the MS was still in her system, but Jillian wasn't about to let her illness infringe on her happiness.

She was more than satisfied to take things one day at a time. Hadn't she told Luanne the same thing? Luanne's case had gotten some help when they'd discovered Eric actually had written proof of Nelson's blackmail. As a result, she was confident her friend would get a lighter sentence.

Life was good. Jillian had taken the first steps to change her focus to study neurology. She was determined to find a cure for MS.

Later that evening, she and Alec finally had a few moments alone on the dance floor.

"I've missed you," he murmured, molding her body against his as they swayed to the music. "I can't wait until we're married and living in the same house."

She wound her arms around his broad shoulders. "Me, too."

Jillian had refused to move in, mostly because of Shelby, wanting to set a good example for the future. Which probably only added to Alec's impatience to be married. She had to admit, sneaking out of his bedroom late at night was getting old.

"How long do you think we have to stay?" Alec asked, glancing around at the wedding reception still in full swing.

"You're the best man," she reminded him. "I'm sure you can last a little longer."

"Maybe," he growled, before trailing a string of hot kisses behind her ear. "Maybe not."

Jillian pulled away so she could see his eyes. The banked desire in the green depths made her want to ditch the wedding reception, too. "I have some news," she said, as a way to distract him.

"Yeah? Good news?" Alec asked, pressing her hips

more snugly against his so that she could feel the hard evidence of his arousal.

"Very good news." She ignored the flash of desire weakening her limbs. She'd waited since yesterday's appointment with Dr. Juran to tell him. "Dr. Juran reassured me there's no reason I can't have children."

Alec stopped, right there in the middle of the dance floor, his gaze probing hers. "Are you sure?"

She nodded, unable to keep from smiling. "Very sure."

"Then we're outta here." Alec gave her a quick kiss. "Let's go."

"Alec!" She laughed as he tried to tug her toward the door. "I didn't mean right this minute."

"I did." He stopped long enough to cradle her cheek in the palm of his hand. "I love you, Jillian. I don't want to wait."

Well, that was just fine with her.

Because neither did she.

MILLS & BOON®

JUNE 2007 HARDBACK TITLES

ROMANCE™

Taken: the Spaniard's Virgin *Lucy Monroe*	978 0 263 19636 8
The Petrakos Bride *Lynne Graham*	978 0 263 19637 5
The Brazilian Boss's Innocent Mistress *Sarah Morgan*	
	978 0 263 19638 2
For the Sheikh's Pleasure *Annie West*	978 0 263 19639 9
The Greek Prince's Chosen Wife *Sandra Marton*	
	978 0 263 19640 5
Bedded at His Convenience *Margaret Mayo*	978 0 263 19641 2
The Billionaire's Marriage Bargain *Carole Mortimer*	
	978 0 263 19642 9
The Greek Billionaire's Baby Revenge *Jennie Lucas*	
	978 0 263 19643 6
The Italian's Wife by Sunset *Lucy Gordon*	978 0 263 19644 3
Reunited: Marriage in a Million *Liz Fielding*	978 0 263 19645 0
His Miracle Bride *Marion Lennox*	978 0 263 19646 7
Break Up to Make Up *Fiona Harper*	978 0 263 19647 4
Marrying Her Billionaire Boss *Myrna Mackenzie*	
	978 0 263 19648 1
Baby Twins: Parents Needed *Teresa Carpenter*	978 0 263 19649 8
The Italian GP's Bride *Kate Hardy*	978 0 263 19650 4
The Doctor's Pregnancy Secret *Leah Martyn*	978 0 263 19651 1

HISTORICAL ROMANCE™

No Place For a Lady *Louise Allen*	978 0 263 19763 1
Bride of the Solway *Joanna Maitland*	978 0 263 19764 8
Marianne and the Marquis *Anne Herries*	978 0 263 19765 5

MEDICAL ROMANCE™

The Consultant's Italian Knight *Maggie Kingsley*	
	978 0 263 19804 1
Her Man of Honour *Melanie Milburne*	978 0 263 19805 8
One Special Night... *Margaret McDonagh*	978 0 263 19806 5
Bride for a Single Dad *Laura Iding*	978 0 263 19807 2

MILLS & BOON®

0507 Gen Std LP

JUNE 2007 LARGE PRINT TITLES

ROMANCE™

Taken by the Sheikh *Penny Jordan*	978 0 263 19455 5
The Greek's Virgin *Trish Morey*	978 0 263 19456 2
The Forced Bride *Sara Craven*	978 0 263 19457 9
Bedded and Wedded for Revenge *Melanie Milburne*	
	978 0 263 19458 6
Rancher and Protector *Judy Christenberry*	978 0 263 19459 3
The Valentine Bride *Liz Fielding*	978 0 263 19460 9
One Summer in Italy... *Lucy Gordon*	978 0 263 19461 6
Crowned: An Ordinary Girl *Natasha Oakley*	978 0 263 19462 3

HISTORICAL ROMANCE™

The Wanton Bride *Mary Brendan*	978 0 263 19394 7
A Scandalous Mistress *Juliet Landon*	978 0 263 19395 4
A Wealthy Widow *Anne Herries*	978 0 263 19396 1

MEDICAL ROMANCE™

The Midwife's Christmas Miracle *Sarah Morgan*	978 0 263 19351 0
One Night To Wed *Alison Roberts*	978 0 263 19352 7
A Very Special Proposal *Josie Metcalfe*	978 0 263 19353 4
The Surgeon's Meant-To-Be Bride *Amy Andrews*	
	978 0 263 19354 1
A Father By Christmas *Meredith Webber*	978 0 263 19551 4
A Mother for His Baby *Leah Martyn*	978 0 263 19552 1

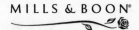

MILLS & BOON®

JULY 2007 HARDBACK TITLES

ROMANCE™

Blackmailed into the Italian's Bed *Miranda Lee* 978 0 263 19652 8
The Greek Tycoon's Pregnant Wife *Anne Mather*
978 0 263 19653 5
Innocent on Her Wedding Night *Sara Craven* 978 0 263 19654 2
The Spanish Duke's Virgin Bride *Chantelle Shaw*
978 0 263 19655 9
The Mediterranean Billionaire's Secret Baby *Diana Hamilton*
978 0 263 19656 6
The Boss's Wife for a Week *Anne McAllister* 978 0 263 19657 3
The Kouros Marriage Revenge *Abby Green* 978 0 263 19658 0
Jed Hunter's Reluctant Bride *Susanne James* 978 0 263 19659 7
Promoted: Nanny to Wife *Margaret Way* 978 0 263 19660 3
Needed: Her Mr Right *Barbara Hannay* 978 0 263 19661 0
Outback Boss, City Bride *Jessica Hart* 978 0 263 19662 7
The Bridal Contract *Susan Fox* 978 0 263 19663 4
Marriage at Circle M *Donna Alward* 978 0 263 19664 1
The Italian Single Dad *Jennie Adams* 978 0 263 19665 8
The Single Dad's Marriage Wish *Carol Marinelli*
978 0 263 19666 5
The Surgeon's Runaway Bride *Olivia Gates* 978 0 263 19667 2

HISTORICAL ROMANCE™

A Desirable Husband *Mary Nichols* 978 0 263 19766 2
His Cinderella Bride *Annie Burrows* 978 0 263 19767 9
Tamed By the Barbarian *June Francis* 978 0 263 19768 6

MEDICAL ROMANCE™

The Playboy Doctor's Proposal *Alison Roberts* 978 0 263 19808 9
The Consultant's Surprise Child *Joanna Neil* 978 0 263 19809 6
Dr Ferrero's Baby Secret *Jennifer Taylor* 978 0 263 19810 2
Their Very Special Child *Dianne Drake* 978 0 263 19811 9

MILLS & BOON®

0607 Gen Std LP

JULY 2007 LARGE PRINT TITLES

ROMANCE™

Royally Bedded, Regally Wedded *Julia James* 978 0 263 19463 0
The Sheikh's English Bride *Sharon Kendrick* 978 0 263 19464 7
Sicilian Husband, Blackmailed Bride *Kate Walker*
978 0 263 19465 4
At the Greek Boss's Bidding *Jane Porter* 978 0 263 19466 1
Cattle Rancher, Convenient Wife *Margaret Way*
978 0 263 19467 8
Barefoot Bride *Jessica Hart* 978 0 263 19468 5
Their Very Special Gift *Jackie Braun* 978 0 263 19469 2
Her Parenthood Assignment *Fiona Harper* 978 0 263 19470 8

HISTORICAL ROMANCE™

Innocence and Impropriety *Diane Gaston* 978 0 263 19397 8
Rogue's Widow, Gentleman's Wife *Helen Dickson*
978 0 263 19398 5
High Seas To High Society *Sophia James* 978 0 263 19399 2

MEDICAL ROMANCE™

The Surgeon's Miracle Baby *Carol Marinelli* 978 0 263 19355 8
A Consultant Claims His Bride *Maggie Kingsley*
978 0 263 19356 5
The Woman He's Been Waiting For *Jennifer Taylor*
978 0 263 19357 2
The Village Doctor's Marriage *Abigail Gordon* 978 0 263 19358 9
In Her Boss's Special Care *Melanie Milburne* 978 0 263 19554 5
The Surgeon's Courageous Bride *Lucy Clark* 978 0 263 19555 2